KEEPING UP APPEARANCES

Ann Roberts

Spinsters Ink
2010

Spinsters Ink
P.O. Box 242
Midway, Florida 32343

Printed in the United States of America on acid-free paper

First Edition

Editor: Katherine V. Forrest
Cover designer: Linda Callaghan

ISBN: 978-1-935226-43-7

About the Author

Ann Roberts's career as a teacher and administrator spans kindergarten to college. She lives in Phoenix with her partner, her son and their two large Rhodesian Ridgebacks, Sadie and Duke, aka "Dukalicious."

She is the author of *Furthest from the Gate* and several Bella Books titles: *Brilliant, Beach Town, Root of Passion, Beacon of Love,* as well as the Ari Adams' mystery series that includes *Paid in Full* and *White Offerings*. She can be reached at her Web site www.annroberts.net.

Author's Note or My Little Rant

Although gay rights have certainly progressed, there's no faster way to start a fight in middle school than to call a boy a "fag" or a "queer." Classroom discussions that evolve into questions about homosexuality are quickly terminated and most gay educators recognize that they are held to a higher standard and even the most liberal communities appreciate a civilian version of "Don't Ask, Don't Tell." Homophobia is truly the last form of accepted prejudice in public education and while the consequences are very clear for racial and religious intolerance, a hazy double standard (okay, it's not so hazy in some parts of the country) is often applied when an issue involving homophobia surfaces. I give a huge shout-out to GLSEN and the thousands of teachers, counselors, parents and administrators who soldier along quietly each day working to change the school culture for our gay students. They are the heroes.

Acknowledgments

Teachers are made, not born. I was inspired by so many of the marvelous men and women I met during my years in school, including my mother, a sixth grade teacher who always knew how to explain everything just right.

Over the last twenty-three years I've been incredibly fortunate to work with some very fine professionals—counselors, special education directors, school psychologists, regular education teachers and special education teachers.

And to the wonderful people around me from whom I learn every day: my partner, Amy, a second-grade teacher; my friend Patricia, a fellow principal and sounding board—who eventually found her "right seat on the bus" (but is not depicted in this story); and of course, my son, who shows me every day how much more there is to learn. I'm hoping that he'll believe the same once he's no longer a teenager...love ya son!

I am grateful for the help I received in the creation of this new work. Katherine V. Forrest supported me tremendously through a difficult rewrite and the editing process. My friend and high school buddy Suemeree kept the "school language" readable, and of course, Linda Hill and Spinsters Ink who continue to make a home for my writing.

"Women teachers who marry or engage in unseemly conduct will be dismissed."
—Rules for Teachers (1872)

"An employee is not wrongfully terminated if he is fired for being a homosexual."
—Arizona Superior Court Judge in *Blaine v. Golden State Container*
(upheld by Arizona Court of Appeals, 1994)

Chapter One

2004

If she was fired, Faye Burton knew she could always get a job at that new place that had just opened, Starbuck's. She'd spent her college years mixing coffee drinks long before employees were called baristas and soy lattés were fashionable.

She gazed out the expansive windows that surrounded her office at Cedar Hills Elementary School, watching the seventh and eighth graders change classes. As the principal she shouldered the responsibility of educating over one thousand students, supervising ninety-eight employees, coddling seven hundred different sets of parents—many of whom were involved in messy divorces—and managing a sixteen million dollar facility. And the rumor at the district office was that the new superintendent wanted her gone because she was gay.

She let out a deep breath and watched the students cross

the courtyard area. A few engaged in playful shoving, unable to keep their hands to themselves, and some boy-girl couples hugged before heading to class. It was only the fourth week of school and halos still hung over most of them. Although a few of the girls were questionably dressed for the one-hundred-and-five degree Phoenix heat, Faye found no reason to jump from her chair and run outside to impose discipline on any of the pre-teenagers.

They entered the buildings and she realized it was nearly ten o'clock—time for her first monthly meeting with the new superintendent, Dr. Bill Gleeson. She'd only met him twice, once at a meet-and-greet before the school year began and at their first administrative meeting.

She remembered the look on his face when she'd offered her hand after the assistant superintendent initially introduced them. His smile cracked slightly as if it was painful to touch her.

"Ms. Burton, I'm pleased to meet you," he'd said woodenly. "Cedar Hills is a school capable of greatness. My secretary will schedule a meeting with you so that we can discuss my vision."

She'd nodded and he'd walked away without another word. She knew what he wanted—higher test results. In the year she'd been there, she'd raised the test scores significantly but it wasn't enough. The school's lackluster performance had forced her predecessor's resignation and she'd inherited a talented but unruly staff that made ridiculous demands and accusations, like the bizarre first-grade teacher who claimed the fax machine was racist. The road of change would take time but she wasn't sure Bill Gleeson would wait. Cedar Hills was a school filled with the sons and daughters of lawyers and doctors, all of whom believed their children were geniuses bound for college.

She popped two antacid tablets and heard a knock at her door. Jonnie Clark stuck her head inside.

"Hey, is now an awful time?"

"It's always a great time for you," she said, instantly cheerful. "What's up?"

Jonnie shut the door and plopped into a chair. She was an amazing school counselor and incredibly mature for thirty. Her body was lean from kickboxing and she often wore retro clothing like bell-bottom pants and knitted sweater vests. She always had a cause and she advertised them on the back of her beat-up Honda Civic.

"I need your help. It seems that an eighth-grade boy peed on a fourth grader."

She threw up her hands. "What? Are you kidding? How did this happen? Were they messing around at the urinal?"

"Actually he was in the next stall. It's kinda freaky…" She made an arch with her index finger and giggled. Faye joined her and they howled until they cried.

Jonnie clapped her hands. "Okay, enough. We've got to get serious. I need you to talk to…" She paused and snapped her fingers. "What's his name?"

"Peeboy," Faye said.

They laughed again. Jonnie took a stress ball from Faye's desk and threw it at her. "C'mon, Faye. We're serious now. This child's been horribly violated."

"You're absolutely right. I'd die if someone peed on me."

They went down the hall to Jonnie's office and interviewed the whimpering fourth grader, determining that he could offer little as a witness. All he'd seen were large black canvas sneakers when he'd looked under the stall so he knew the kid was much older. He left and a sweet acrid scent filled the room. Jonnie thrust a paper in Faye's direction.

"What's this?"

"It's a requisition for a case of air freshener and I'd better not hear any crap about it."

Faye had just returned to her office when her radio squawked. "Office, I need a wheelchair in the gym, stat!"

"What's going on, Coach?" she asked, bolting out the back door toward the gym.

"Third grader down," Coach Fleming responded.

Faye glanced over her shoulder and saw Nurse Chang hustling across the courtyard, pushing a wheelchair. Inside the gym a little girl with pigtails writhed on the floor, cradling her right arm. The rest of the class hovered nearby and her friends wailed in sympathy for their fallen classmate.

Faye said into the radio, "Front office, send Ms. Clark down here immediately. I've got a room full of crying students." She turned to Coach Fleming, a fifty-something bull-dyke with a pompadour hairstyle. "What happened?"

She shrugged with the complacency of a veteran teacher. "She was climbing the rope and lost her grip." No other explanation was necessary.

As they wheeled the student back to the nurse's office, Faye heard the ambulance in the distance. By the time they'd called the parent, the paramedics had arrived. Faye stepped out of the way and heard shouting.

Assistant Principal Pete Salinas burst into the lobby, followed by a screaming woman who quickly gained the attention of the other adults nearby. She waved a pink paper in her hand, which Faye knew was a disciplinary referral.

"You fucking spic! How dare you suspend my kid?"

Pete crossed his arms and stared her down. "Ma'am, this conversation is over. I will not tolerate such blatant racism."

"I'm going to the district office, you stupid wetback! Let's see if you have a job at four o'clock!"

The woman turned on her heel and nearly ran into Bill Gleeson, who stood like a tree. His neutral expression never changed as she huffed past him. He seemed not to notice her or the stretcher that flew out the door, surrounded by three paramedics. His gaze remained locked on Faye, who turned to Pete.

"I take it that didn't go too well."

Pete grinned and Faye saw the twinkle in his eye. He loved confrontation with unreasonable parents.

"I see you have company," he said. "Have fun."

Faye painted on her pleasant expression and greeted Gleeson. Once they were sequestered in her office she made a joke to lighten the mood.

"Well, Bill, you've just seen elementary school at its most interesting."

Shit. I just called him Bill.

He withdrew his gold pen from his breast pocket and made some notes while she sat in the awkward silence, listening to the pen scratch against the paper.

"I assume this is an unusual morning, Ms. Burton."

She chuckled. "Somewhat."

"You seem to have more than most," he said blandly.

She shifted in her seat. "What do you mean?"

He shuffled through some papers on the clipboard until he found one close to the bottom. "According to our records, my office has received *five* parent complaints since the beginning of the year and the union has filed an official grievance on behalf of a teacher about her evaluation from last year. Most important," he said, withdrawing a memo, "Constance Richardson has called the state department of education to complain that Cedar Hills is prejudiced against her son Armour and trying to force him out because of his special needs. She's demanding that his opportunities be expanded and that he be placed in a physical education class. She faxed this complaint to Andrea Loomis, our new special education director, and threatened to file it with the state and go to the media."

Faye scanned the memo and shook her head. The back of her neck felt hot. "This is entirely baseless."

He looked at her curiously. "Is it?"

"Yes," she said, defensively. "Constance Richardson regularly makes our lives miserable, but A.J. as we call him, doesn't even belong at Cedar Hills and certainly not in a P.E. class. He's a danger to the campus," she added.

Gleeson wrote down her statement on his pad but showed no reaction and eventually said, "I've asked our new special education director, Ms. Loomis, to visit with you about this situation. It needs to go away."

"I wish it were that easy. Ms. Richardson is a high-powered attorney who's never been told no."

Gleeson didn't respond and his gaze returned to his clipboard. "I'm confident Ms. Loomis can take care of this."

He returned to scratching the paper and more silence ensued. She glanced around her office, suddenly wondering how many boxes she would need to pack her personal belongings. He checked a few more notes and cleared his throat.

"Do you have a response for the other complaints?"

"No. There will always be parents who don't like the fact

that we hold their children accountable. Mr. Salinas has the unpleasant task of handling discipline and he is frequently the target of abuse."

"Would you say Mr. Salinas is competent at his job?"

"Absolutely. He's one of the best assistant principals that I've ever known."

Gleeson checked his notes again. "Hmm. Well, he has more suspensions than any other AP and most of those complaints I mentioned before involve *him*. I've also found him to have a… how can I put this? A rather unpolished demeanor."

Her eyebrows shot up. "Excuse me?"

He carefully set his pen down on the clipboard and faced her directly. He smoothed his silk tie, displaying his perfect manicure. "Ms. Burton, I'm going to get right to the point. I have concerns about the leadership of this school. While I do believe you and Mr. Salinas are competent educators, I'm not sure that you can effectively project the image that I feel is necessary to move Cedar Hills to the level of the other schools."

She narrowed her eyes and held his gaze. He sat across from her in a dark blue suit that she imagined was tailor-made. There was not a lint ball visible and his tie was perfectly knotted. She didn't dare look down at her thirty dollar cotton pants or her Sears button-down shirt. And she knew that if Pete appeared at the door, Gleeson would automatically frown at his rumpled pants, stained tie and disheveled hair that always seemed to fall in his face. Clearly she and Pete would never win best-dressed awards.

"If that's your impression then I welcome your suggestions to improve the *image* of Cedar Hills. I'm sure Mr. Salinas would as well."

He nodded once, his chin lowering just enough to make the gesture visible, and then asked to see some classrooms.

They walked in and out of the various wings, Gleeson scribbling on his pad and ignoring Faye.

As they stood in Ruby Taylor's art class, watching the seventh-and-eighth grade students create watercolor paintings, she calculated her monthly bills, reviewing the steps to make a double-shot espresso. He was out to get her and if Constance

Richardson filed a complaint with the state, he would gladly provide the moving boxes for her.

Once they'd left the art class Gleeson turned to her, his finger pointed, as if he was about to begin a lecture. A shrill cry tore through the hallway. The door to the art room burst open and two figures poured out, a boy holding a colorful picture and a girl chasing after him. In a second Faye realized what was happening and stepped out of the child's path, but Gleeson, the interloper, remained rooted in place. Before Faye could pull him aside, the yellows, reds and greens of the watercolor pressed against his powder-blue shirt and the boy crashed to the floor.

"Oh, my God," the girl wailed.

Gleeson stared at the mess on his chest and looked at Faye, his expression unforgiving.

Faye turned her gaze to the girl in black jeans and a Melissa Etheridge T-shirt. She was rail-thin and her uneven spiky haircut was definitely a home job.

"Pandy, what happened?"

"He got upset because Ms. Taylor said it was time to cleanup."

All three of them stared at the boy, who, although he was only a year younger than Pandy, was much smaller than the other seventh graders. Pandy held him in place and he stared at his ruined painting. She whispered to him and he nodded. When he looked up, he strained his neck dramatically to see Bill Gleeson's face, which must have seemed a mile away.

"Dr. Gleeson, I'd like you to meet Pandy Webber, one of our student mentors, and this is her mentee, A.J. Richardson."

Gleeson shot her a knowing glare but said nothing.

"I'm sorry, Ms. Burton," Pandy said. "He ran out so fast."

"It's okay, Pandy. I'm sure you did your best to stop him."

A.J. laughed and pointed at Gleeson's shirt, the wet paint reminding Faye of a bad Picasso. He threw the picture in the air and cried, "Fasty native!"

Chapter Two

Constance Richardson hated mornings. Although she was highly skilled in the art of persuasion, none of her tactics could motivate her son to *quickly* prepare for school. Each day she coaxed and prodded him to get ready for the bus that stopped in front of their high-rise condominium. If he missed it she would be saddled with the task of putting him in her car, driving to Cedar Hills and cajoling him from the vehicle. This would require her to cancel her first appointment of the morning and forfeit one to two billable hours from her weekly timesheet. Thank God she was the boss at *Constance Richardson, Attorney at Law, LLP.*

She'd reviewed her Blackberry and her day would start promptly at eight with a client interview, followed by a meeting with the new special education director and a showdown with the unsuspecting husband of her most high-maintenance client.

"And all before lunch," she murmured.

"Cut the crusts off, Mommy," Armour whined as he climbed up on the counter next to her. She winced when his index finger probed his right nostril.

"Armour, don't pick your nose."

"I don't like the crusts."

"The crusts are good for you," she said, repeating the same wisdom her mother had imparted to her.

She glanced at her frowning son. He was twelve but he was small and immature enough to jump on the kitchen counter, unaware that his left hand rested in a stray drop of maple syrup that had missed his breakfast plate. He inevitably would wipe the syrup on his tan Dockers and the stain would be the first of many during the day, ensuring that by three o'clock his new outfit was covered in food and snot, and his sporty haircut, after a day of scratching his head, would be like a used mop.

She grimaced and reminded herself that he couldn't help it. He was autistic and technically not her son—but her nephew. She'd inherited him after her sister's death and there was little she could do to change his behavior. Lesser people would call him damaged goods and in her most shameful moments of frustration with him, the phrase raced through her mind.

He hopped off the counter and went to his room while she searched the kitchen drawers for a sandwich bag. Normally he ate the cafeteria food or a lunch prepared by Cathy, his nanny. But she was late and Constance knew Armour wouldn't stomach the nachos and cheese that was on the school's menu. She sighed. She shouldn't complain. Her own mother had performed all of these domestic duties with a perpetual smile on her face.

"You and your sister are the lights of our lives," June Richardson had said every morning, and their father would grin from behind his paper.

Buck Richardson wasn't much of a talker. He was a simple man who loved his daughters and adored his wife. He may have been the breadwinner but June was the boss, and when Constance summoned any memory of her early childhood, it always brought a smile to her face. They had been such a happy family—for a while.

Armour raced back into the kitchen and stared at the sandwich. "Mommy, you didn't cut off the crusts. I don't want the crusts!" he screamed, pounding on the counter. "No crusts! No crusts!"

"Armour, you will eat this sandwich the way I have prepared it."

"Uh-uh. Uh-uh." He shook his head back and forth so fiercely that she thought he might hurt his neck.

"Yes," she answered firmly, pointing at him, attempting to gain his attention.

He frowned, grabbed the sandwich and hurled it across the room. It smashed against the back of the sofa, jelly dripping toward the crème carpet.

"Fasty native!" he cried.

He ran around the couch, waving his arms and screeching. After three laps he disappeared into his room and slammed the door.

She closed her eyes and summoned a vision of her mother, standing in the kitchen, carefully preparing her daughters' lunches while they ate breakfast at the nearby table, listening to her sing a Cole Porter song, usually "You do Something to Me."

When Constance's anger subsided, she reached for her Blackberry and sent a text to her secretary, instructing her to reschedule her eight o'clock meeting with the new client. As she grabbed a sponge and mopped the bleeding jelly from the expensive Italian leather, she could still hear her mother's voice.

Constance glanced at her Rolex as she waited on the hideous loveseat outside of Andrea Loomis's office. No doubt scoundrels, gangbangers and other filthy miscreants had sat on these cushions that touched her Armani suit now. She grimaced. Loomis was ten minutes late and time was money in Constance's world, a concept that educators never seemed to grasp.

Three minutes later she was ushered down a tiny hallway—past an array of cubicles that housed the bureaucratic grunts who ate up her tax dollars—and into Loomis's tiny office. At least she got a window.

The woman who greeted her wasn't what she expected. Her shoulder-length blond hair was pulled away from her striking face and fastened with a clip, but the front strands deliberately rested against her high cheekbones. It was an eloquent look and Constance imagined she often caught the eye of any man in a meeting. She wore a gold pinky ring and several expensive gold bracelets adorned her right wrist. Constance was immediately impressed by her dark blue Prada suit and her matching Manolo Blanhik heels.

"Ms. Richardson, I'm Andrea Loomis."

Her handshake was firm and she made direct eye contact, two behaviors that instantly activated Constance's radar. This woman wasn't a pushover.

"Ms. Loomis, I appreciate you seeing me."

They sat down and sized each other up like two animals of prey circling, Constance thought.

Loomis smiled pleasantly and said, "Let's see if we can resolve some of the concerns you have about your son."

"I won't take up much of your time. This visit is merely a courtesy at the request of Dr. Gleeson. He hopes that we can smooth out our differences before I file my complaint with the state."

Loomis glanced at her copy of the complaint. "If I understand correctly, you believe Ms. Burton wishes to force A.J. from Cedar Hills, thus depriving him of his least restrictive environment."

Constance nodded. "That's correct. If Armour is to leave Cedar Hills, I must agree to it. That's the terms of his plan."

"Who agreed to these terms?" Loomis asked, almost scowling.

"The team," she said, referring to the group that oversaw Armour's education. It included herself, Faye Burton, Armour's classroom teacher, Mrs. Strauss, and the previous special education director who was a spineless whiner. "And," she quickly added, "Dr. Marjorie."

Loomis's shoulders sagged and Constance suppressed a smile. Assistant Superintendent Dr. Marjorie Machabell was her ace, a marshmallow who kept the parents happy at any cost and jumped anytime she was threatened with poor press. Apparently Ms. Loomis had already learned in her short tenure with the Glen Oaks School District that Dr. Marjorie was the weak link.

Loomis studied the document and said slowly, "I understand the original conditions but surely you'd reconsider if changing your son's placement was in his best interest. I've read over his file and his antics are rather outrageous, including a time where he flung himself off the stage trying to fly. Based on these incidences Ms. Burton believes he doesn't belong in a P.E. class where there's a lot of activity and she questions his placement at Cedar Hills. And honestly, I see her point. Wouldn't it be better to put him in a small environment where he can be closely watched?"

Constance leaned forward and stared at her. "Hear me, Ms. Loomis. Armour will never leave Cedar Hills. Period. If you try to force me out, you'll be dealing with a lawsuit and some very nasty press. I'm certain Superintendent Gleeson doesn't want to begin his career at Glen Oaks with a black cloud."

Loomis leaned back in her chair and crossed her arms. "Ms. Richardson, are you threatening me?" A slight Texas twang escaped with the question. "I don't respond well to ultimatums and at some point you may need me. I haven't spoken yet with Ms. Burton but A.J.'s behavior—"

"Please don't call him A.J. That's the cutesy little nickname they've given him. His name is Armour."

She took a breath and nodded. "*Armour's* behavior is unpredictable and unpredictable children can cause problems, sometimes *legal* problems for their parents."

Loomis winked and smiled, and when Constance looked down, her hands were shaking. She was grateful when Loomis's secretary interrupted with the old ploy of an important phone call sitting on hold.

She stood to go. "I know you're very busy so I'll be blunt. I'm unhappy with Armour's education at Cedar Hills, an education he is entitled to have. If I don't receive some *evidence* that things will change, I'll file that complaint shortly."

She didn't wait for Loomis to reply but quickly left with the last word, hoping that her voice hadn't quaked from the seed of fear that Andrea Loomis had planted.

By the time she returned to her office she was in control again, an unrelenting force that flattened anything in her way. Her colleagues had nicknamed her the Steamroller. Once she finished with an opponent he usually felt two-dimensional. She was known for her lucrative divorce settlements that transformed unhappy wives into filthy rich divorcees who could afford every luxury imaginable. The philandering assholes who had wronged their brides were lucky to escape with enough cash to support an apartment and the mistress who'd usually caused the divorce in the first place.

Melanie presented her with three messages and said her client was running ten minutes late.

"Too bad for her. Bill her the time," she said before retreating into her office.

A designer's masterpiece, she'd told her decorator that she wanted to make a powerful and intimidating first impression. The fabulous lines of the mahogany furniture and the plush leather sofas and chairs humbled the most arrogant visitors. The surroundings proved to be an inevitable conversation starter for all of her clients who praised her tasteful artwork, her collection of Dale Chihuly glass and the breathtaking view of South Mountain that could be seen from an expansive bank of windows behind her desk. After their effusive praise and predictable questions, she'd billed at least ten minutes to their account simply because they couldn't stay on point.

She dropped her leather portfolio on the ten thousand dollar Italian desk and detoured into her private bathroom to check her face in the mirror. The flattering lighting was kind, a design she'd insisted upon when she rented the office space. The lines around her mouth were returning, as Dr. Haskell had said they would four years ago when she'd gone in for a little work. Otherwise her face remained loyal after forty-seven years and she wore no trace of her past.

She leaned toward the mirror until her breath kissed the glass, staring at the pores on her face, no longer worried about her age, but remembering a day long ago when she'd stared into a mirror and fled her old life forever.

She'd married her college sweetheart as a way to escape her father Buck, who'd become abusive after her mother June died from cancer. He was happy to give her to Earl, believing that she and her sister Cora were deadweights that needed food and clothing. But life in a double-wide outside of Atwood, Kansas, wasn't enough. One day as she was getting ready for her shift at the diner, she stared into the cracked mirror and adjusted her scarf, just as a passing cloud eclipsed the afternoon sun and darkness filled the bedroom. It passed quickly but in those few seconds she saw her life for what it was. She suppressed an urge to strangle herself with the scarf and instead filled a suitcase with her clothes and Earl's Saturday night fun money.

She fled to Nate Palmer, the high school counselor who'd always told her she could fulfill her dreams. He was much older but they became lovers. He agreed to finance her education at Kansas State in exchange for her companionship.

Quid pro quo, he would say, a legal expression meaning something for something. She took it to heart. She never expected something for nothing and she demanded the same in return. It was an arrangement that suited both of them for the next seven years until she graduated from college and law school. Nate was her Svengali, expanding her horizons, providing her with unbelievable opportunities and teaching her the fine art of control.

When he died of a heart attack three years after she'd moved to Phoenix, he bequeathed a sizeable inheritance to her and she started her own company. Within five years she'd attained all of the trappings that proved she'd arrived—an office downtown, Jaguar and a posh condo on Central Avenue. She was achieving her professional milestones at breakneck speed. Then Armour arrived after Cora's death. And Constance owed Cora everything.

She pointed at the mirror. "*Everything*," she reminded herself. "Quid pro quo."

She reapplied her lipstick and straightened her jacket before returning to her desk and the case file. Zoe Manos was an up-and-coming chef who had opened a premier Greek restaurant the year before. After falling in love with her sommelier, she needed to shed the milquetoast husband who had supported her through cooking school, often playing breadwinner and nanny to their two adorable children while she studied appetizers through desserts. Constance knew the husband's attorney would press for joint custody and half of the assets, but Zoe, never one accustomed to sharing, wanted it all and Constance had a plan to make that happen.

Zoe was a whiny, self-absorbed Greek princess who'd gotten everything she wanted from every man in her life—her father, her husband and her lover. Constance almost felt sorry for Nick Manos. It wasn't just the nice girls who chose foolishly. There were plenty of men who picked the beautiful bitch over the astounding yet average woman. She reached into her desk drawer for a key and unlocked the credenza behind her. Her fingers trailed across the tabs until she found the hanging file labeled Caliente Investigations. She withdrew a manila envelope and placed it behind the papers in the Manos folder before joining her client.

Zoe sat in the conference room, chewing on a wad of gum and shaking her foot nervously. Ten minutes later Nick Manos rushed in with his lawyer following behind. She immediately sized up the attorney. While Manos was dressed in jeans and a T-shirt, the handsome attorney wore chinos, a button-down shirt and a rumpled jacket. His five o'clock shadow was about forty hours old and it seemed combing his curly black hair was optional. He was probably in his early to mid-thirties, smart and sharp, and he didn't need a three-piece suit to prove it.

"Sorry we're late," he said, setting his scuffed briefcase on the perfectly polished glass conference table. "I'm Ira Leibowitz."

"Constance Richardson."

She proffered her hand and was met with a firm handshake that emitted confidence but a cognizance that the recipient was delicate, feminine. She immediately guessed that he was an exceptional lover. He turned to Zoe and nodded before settling next to Manos. She watched Manos's eyes, full of hatred, never leaving his soon-to-be ex-wife's face. Zoe stared beyond the conference room's large glass door toward Constance's busy employees swirling in activity. She appeared totally bored.

"Well, we should get right to it," Leibowitz said with a pleasant smile. He opened his briefcase and pulled out a sheaf of papers. "We've prepared what we believe is a very fair settlement, given the fact that my client supported his wife through school. We think that he should reap some of the rewards of her success, considering that he helped make it happen."

He offered the papers to Constance, who remained still, her face neutral, her gaze locked on his blue eyes. He was so young, so naïve and so well-meaning. Of course he was right. Manos should get half of everything but he wouldn't. He should probably have sole custody of the children given Zoe's work schedule and selfishness, but Constance's efforts on her client's behalf ensured that the two adorable children would spend most of their time with a nanny while Mommy worked or screwed her new lover.

And she loved the element of surprise. Usually she savored the negotiations, the turmoil, and in the end, the kill. But today she wanted to skip the foreplay and move right to the climax. Maybe Leibowitz would join her for lunch.

When she refused to accept the papers, he dropped them on the table and leaned back in his chair. "I assume you have your own proposal? By all means, I apologize. Ladies first."

"Actually, Mr. Leibowitz, Mr. Manos, I have the *only* proposal." She opened her case file and withdrew the contents of the manila envelope, five eight-by-ten photographs. "These pictures are so clear," she commented, as she handed them to Leibowitz.

Manos leaned over to see the first picture and his face fell when he recognized himself—dancing in a gay bar, shirtless, another man behind him wearing only a Speedo, licking his ear and pushing his hands down the front of Manos's jeans.

He slumped into his chair and wept. His self-absorbed, rich and nearly divorced wife didn't even hand him a tissue.

Chapter Three

"Pandy, you forgot the back side." A.J. quickly flipped over the math paper and she smiled weakly. "Why aren't you helping?" he asked in his perturbed voice.

For a boy who wasn't all there he could be quite perceptive. He always knew her moods, and one day when she'd come to school drunk, he was the one who asked, "Why does your breath smell funny?" when all of her teachers had failed to notice.

She was definitely distracted. While A.J. studied the problems, Pandy pulled the printed e-mail message from her pocket and read it again. It was from her mother, who rarely wrote to her, but she was coming to Phoenix for Christmas with her new family and she wanted to see Pandy.

An image of boiling water pouring over a glass of ice cubes flashed in her mind. She was the ice and Mama was the water, smothering her until she melted. She'd seen her only twice in the last four years after the judge's ruling. She could still see the writing on the decree. *The state of Utah decrees that it is in the best interest of the minor, Pandora Webber, to live with her maternal grandfather in Arizona.* It was in her *best interest* after *the incident* and after she'd tried to kill herself.

She pulled at the thick leather bracelets she wore on both wrists. They were highly fashionable but they served a much greater purpose—they hid the scars left from the suicide attempt.

And lately they covered the fresh cuts she made with her razor blade. The sight of her own blood fascinated her. It always had. She remembered when she was seven she'd stepped on a piece of glass in the trailer's kitchen. Mama had dropped a wine bottle and apparently missed some of the shards. She'd sat in the kitchen studying the red trail drip from her foot, squeezing out the blood until it stung. It was hard to believe that just beneath the thick layers of epidermis lay an entirely differently world, one of color and pain. Then Mama had walked in half-drunk and screamed at the sight. Pandy wasn't sure if Mama had been mad about the floor or scared that she was hurt.

She couldn't decide if she wanted to see Mama but the visit was still two months away. Maybe Mama was going to take her home to be with her new husband and the twins? She doubted it. She couldn't imagine Mama ever wanting her again. She knew she wasn't right.

She flipped over the e-mail and stared at the drawing she'd made during history class. A row of wilting flowers surrounded a fresh grave, a weeping child sitting next to the tombstone. She glanced at the drawing and a weight settled on her shoulders, like a heavy backpack. She wasn't okay, not totally. Her center was rotten and needed to be excised, just as her science teacher Mr. Smith explained when he talked about cancerous tumors. Still…

A.J. rapped his pencil on the desk, a sign of his agitation. She broke away from her thoughts and pointed to one of the problems. His head sunk again and he scratched the paper furiously.

She had worked in A.J.'s special needs class for the past three semesters and she always looked forward to Tuesdays, the day she got to miss P.E. and visit Mrs. Strauss, who always assigned her to help A.J.

It was Ms. Clark who'd asked her to be a student mentor but at first she'd said no. And then Ms. Clark kept asking and she finally decided to try it just to make her happy. She'd spent two years in Ms. Clark's group for gay kids and Ms. Clark knew she'd been taken away from Mama and that she was a cutter. She figured the invitation was out of pity but Ms. Clark insisted that Pandy had a way with people and she was the right kind of person to be a mentor.

Mentoring proved to be one of the only things that she enjoyed about eighth grade, next to being in Ms. Clark's group on Friday mornings. She loved Ms. Clark, Mrs. Strauss, her best friend Brian and A.J. Everything else at Cedar Hills was shit. She hated her worthless classes that forced her to memorize ridiculous details like Civil War battles, algebraic formulas and the periodic table. Only her English teacher Ms. Adams made any sense. They had read *Catcher in the Rye* and she thought the main character could've been her brother. She'd read the book four times, aced the test and earned an A on the thematic essay. Then they started reading some piece of crap, *The Scarlet Letter*, and she tuned out. She hated learning about Puritan America, especially since she couldn't see much difference between the beliefs of seventeen-fifty and the twenty-first century. Her grades weren't so great but they'd let her go to high school and that was all that mattered.

She glanced at A.J. hovering over his paper with his pencil tightly gripped between his fingers, quietly singing the theme song of his favorite cartoon show, *Mr. Zex*. His blond head bopped up and down to the tune and it was hard to believe that they were almost the same age. He wiped his nose on the sleeve of his Abercrombie shirt and she handed him a tissue, which he absently blotted his nose against before returning to his work. He was deep in concentration as he attempted his addition. Suddenly his body froze and he sat up, frowning. He'd hit a mental wall and she needed to help him.

"A.J., what else do you have to do?"

She pointed to the math problem he'd just completed. She saw the simple mistake, one that he wouldn't mind correcting for her, although if Mrs. Strauss asked him to change it, he'd probably throw a temper tantrum and rip off his clothes. Even Mrs. Strauss acknowledged that A.J. listened to Pandy more than he listened to her.

He studied the paper where her finger tapped and immediately began erasing the answer.

"Big mistake," he mumbled. "I'll fix it, Pandy."

She knew not to congratulate him for the correction or show him the other errors. He only could handle fixing one mistake during the math period. There was no point in discussing the many other mistakes he'd made because he would lose it and Mrs. Strauss would need to put him in the area that had been built especially for those times when he couldn't function and became dangerous to the other children. Pandy didn't know why but it seemed that his mother was able to get lots of special things for him. She knew Mrs. Strauss didn't get along with his mom. She'd overheard Mrs. Strauss talking to Principal Burton one day on the phone.

"She thinks he's the only one. She doesn't care that there are six other children in this class, Faye. She's a complete bitch."

Pandy had stepped away when she'd heard Mrs. Strauss swear. That wasn't like her at all. She'd only met Ms. Richardson once when she'd visited the class to observe A.J. working. Unfortunately he'd freaked out when she appeared and ran around the room shrieking and tearing up the worksheets that other students were completing. Finally his mother dragged him out, her arms gripping his shoulders and propelling him forward.

Pandy felt sorry for A.J. She knew he couldn't control his outbursts and that he was different from the other kids—too different. She'd never say it out loud to anyone because she loved him, but she really didn't think he belonged at Cedar Hills.

"Pandy?" A.J. asked.

"Huh?"

He'd stopped working on his math and was coloring the

edges of his paper with a red crayon. He was making flowers. *Like the wildflowers that swayed in the wind.* Her thoughts drifted to that summer in Utah. She saw Athena's little head bob up and down as she toddled across the field.

He giggled and her attention went back to the paper that was covered with his drawings. It was not appropriate and Mrs. Strauss would be upset with any other student who used math time for coloring but Pandy knew he was an exception and he was often allowed to do what others couldn't.

"Pandy," A.J. persisted, "do you have a boyfriend?"

She looked at his serious expression. She wanted to answer honestly but she doubted he could handle the whole truth. "No, A.J., I don't."

He cocked his head to the side and smiled broadly. It was the smile a six-year-old offered when posing for a picture. Of course A.J. was nearly thirteen.

"You're pretty," he said. "You should have a boyfriend. My mom had a boyfriend and then they had a fight and he left. But you should have one too."

"Thanks, A.J. Why don't you draw something for me?" she asked, attempting to change the subject.

"You need a boyfriend," he repeated.

"Hey."

She looked up and smiled. Brian, her best friend and another mentor, dropped into the chair next to them. "Hey," she said. "Aren't you suspended or something?"

He rolled his eyes and wrapped his black trench coat around his body. He was skeletally thin and pale and she knew he wore the coat to look bigger and more threatening.

"Technically I am but since my mom works, she wants me suspended in-school so it's not like a vacation."

He pantomimed quotation marks around the last word and she laughed. He'd been suspended for the second or third time. She couldn't keep track. He refused to be bullied. All of the jocks constantly picked on him because he was gay and he wouldn't take it. He always fought back and he always got suspended.

"I can't believe Mr. Salinas punished you. It was all Travis's fault. He pushed you first."

Travis Ingersoll was the star forward of the Cedar Hills basketball team. During the past season he'd scored more points than any other athlete in Cedar Hills' history. Pandy was also sure he held the record for most students bullied.

"He thinks Travis is perfect," she added. "Just because he's a jock."

Brian shook his head and laughed. "No, he doesn't. He knows what he is. He got suspended too. And Salinas did me a favor. He put me in here with Strauss to help. He knows I love being a mentor. Now I just get to do it for the next three days." He leaned closer and whispered, "I think he did it because Ms. Burton's on our team."

Pandy looked at him surprised. "What?"

"She's a lesbian. Haven't you ever noticed the way she dresses?"

Pandy rolled her eyes. "Brian, just because she doesn't wear skirts or makeup doesn't mean she's a lesbian. Lots of teachers dress down. Look at Mrs. Krumworth. She practically wears her pajamas to school and I *know* she's not a lesbian. I've seen her icky husband with her at the mall."

"Yeah, but Mrs. K's just a teacher. Ms. Burton's a principal. It's different."

She just shook her head. Brian loved to guess who was gay and he was convinced half of the teachers were at least bisexual.

A.J. looked up from his paper. "Brian, are you Pandy's boyfriend?"

He cracked a grin. "No, A.J. I'm Pandy's *best* friend."

"She needs a boyfriend," A.J. said.

She picked up a crayon and added pink swirls to the drawing. "Help me, A.J."

"Who's your boyfriend?" he asked louder, waving his fists in the air. "Boyfriend, boyfriend! Ha! Ha!"

Mrs. Strauss stood up from the table where she was helping another student and stared at them.

Pandy touched his wrist and he immediately deflated, his gaze glued to her arm. She waited until his huge brown eyes looked into hers.

"A.J., I don't have a boyfriend because I don't want one."

Her answer seemed to surprise him and he folded his hands on the table. His shoulders sagged and he frowned as if she'd just delivered the worst news in the world. "Why?"

She glanced at Brian and whispered to A.J., "I won't ever have a boyfriend because I'd rather have a girlfriend."

His brow furrowed and he held his breath as he processed what she had said. She watched him carefully, aware that his explosions often followed these periods of silence. His chest rose and fell as he gasped for air and she thought he might be having a seizure.

"A.J., are you okay?"

The gasps turned to maniacal laughter that overtook his body, like an open Jack-in-the-Box. He twitched in the chair, laughing and shaking. Suddenly he stopped and locked his gaze on her, a wide grin on his face.

"Fasty native!" he proclaimed.

Chapter Four

Faye's drive to work was usually fifteen minutes of pregame strategizing as she prepared for the day. Of course her plans were usually shanghaied by parents and students but that made the job interesting. She'd just organized her morning when her cell phone rang. It was her brother Rob.

"It's awfully early," she answered.

"I know. Look, I want you to meet this permanent sub that's working at my school."

Faye rolled her eyes. "Not again. The last woman you set me up with was twenty-four. I'm forty-one, bro. I want someone who knows that Paul McCartney was in a band *before* Wings and actually owned bell-bottom pants."

"No, no. This woman would be great. She's an academic. She's writing her dissertation on urban societies and she's subbing on the side."

Faye sighed. As a high school history teacher Rob met many women, some of whom were gay and single. He saw each one as a potential date for his old-biddy, lesbian spinster sister. He steered clear of the straight ones, having been financially castrated by a woman he only referred to as the dragon lady.

"Urban societies?" Faye asked. "Sounds really interesting."

"Oh, come on, sis. There's always something. Too young, too old, too butch, too femme—"

"That's not true. I've *never* said too femme," she corrected. She was incredibly attracted to women who were her opposite and relished skirts, lipstick and perfume.

"True, but when was the last time you had a date?"

She rubbed her chin and turned in to the school's parking lot. "Let's see. The last time you fixed me up was with that actress, Light Eternity."

He sighed heavily. "That was only her stage name. Her real name was Marla, remember? The point is you don't date. And if you think I'm going to spend my golden years playing cards with you at a gay senior center, you're crazy. You need to meet someone and stop hiding behind your endless activities."

"Thank you, Dr. Phil. I love you, bro, but don't try so hard. And I promise that if I never meet anyone I won't call you to play cards with me. I'll ask Mr. Greenbaum."

"Who's Mr. Greenbaum?"

"Undoubtedly the little old man who'll live next to me. I'm sure he'll smell of menthol and continually forget to put in his teeth. It'll be delightful. Have you talked to Sau?"

Rob groaned. "Yes."

After his divorce Rob had decided all he could handle was online dating with women who lived far away. Sau was his current connection who lived in the Far East.

"She sent me a biography of Churchill and a book on Richter's work for my birthday."

"Sounds like a very thoughtful gift."

"That part was great," he agreed, "but she also sent me thirty different brochures on Hong Kong."

"Oh. I guess it's time to catch a plane or hit delete on e-mail, huh?"

"Thanks for the metaphor. I'm just not ready, you know?"

"Honey, you're talking to someone who's entirely in touch with that emotion. Why do you think I've never lived with anyone?"

"No, in your case it's because you lack direction and commitment. I'm just afraid of hooking up with a female Dracula."

Faye noticed her secretary standing outside the front door, obviously waiting for her arrival. "I've gotta go, bro. I'll talk to you later."

She piled out of the truck and met Marian. "What's going on?"

"I didn't want to tell you in front of the office staff but Superintendent Gleeson has been here already this morning."

Faye stopped abruptly. "It's not even seven o'clock. What was he doing?"

"I'm not sure but he did ask to use the phone in your office."

She couldn't believe it. She pictured Gleeson burrowing through her drawers, probably looking for a strap-on dildo or some porno videos—anything to short-circuit her career. She quickly archived the items in her desk. In addition to the usual assortment of office supplies, Gleeson could help himself to her antacid pills, aspirin or tampons. He would undoubtedly get a thrill from her treasure drawer, where she kept her confiscated knives, shock buzzers, matches and lighters.

"How long was he here?"

"Not long. After he made his phone call he wandered around the campus for a little while before he came by my desk and said goodbye."

"Great."

Nothing seemed out of place in her office. She fired up her computer and had only answered a dozen e-mails before her cell phone sang, "Ding Dong the Witch is Dead."

She sighed and pressed TALK while she multitasked and responded to a question from one of her teachers. "Hello, Elise. I'm really busy right now. At *work*."

"I know, Faye, but this couldn't wait. I need to ask you a

huge favor. Mitch and I are hosting the annual fall banquet at the club next weekend and we're short a person at our table. It won't look good if we're off-balanced so I was wondering if you were free."

"I'm not sure," she said, giving her standard answer. "I'll need to check my calendar. I'll call you back tonight. I gotta go."

"Wait! I need to know now."

Faye stopped typing. "Why?" Elise stammered and Faye's suspicions grew. "Elise, spill."

"Oh, Faye, can't I just enjoy the pleasure of your company?"

"Please. The last time I went to your club I got into a shouting match with the president because he thought women shouldn't be allowed in the dining room. Do you remember that? When he started talking about the good old days?"

"Mr. Gorman is from a different time—"

"Yes, the chauvinist period." She heard the radio squawk. Someone was calling her name. "Elise, really, people are calling me. Why do you want me there?"

After a long pause Elise finally said, "Okay, the truth is that Fletcher Shanks is in town and I remember what a great time the two of you had together at the Christmas party last year."

Faye almost laughed out loud. Elise was trying to set her up—with one of the gayest men she'd ever met and the stepson of the awful, antiquated president. She and Fletcher had indeed enjoyed the evening together after leaving the stuffy country club—by going to a drag show. Fletcher had stripped down to his underwear, nipple rings and all, and gyrated on top of a table until he fell off. She'd taken him home and they'd talked until sunrise about the difficulty of coming out. Fletcher's mother and Mr. Gorman were in the dark but so was Elise. And Faye still couldn't find the words to tell her oldest sibling that she'd never dated a man and never would.

"Of course I'll come," she said quickly, knowing that she'd enjoy another evening with Fletcher despite Elise's motives.

"That's fabulous!" Elise cooed. "Fletcher and his mother will be thrilled. We'll see you at the club on the twenty-sixth at eight. Ta-ta."

She silenced her phone as the radio squawked again. "Ms. Burton, you're needed in the parking lot."

Faye's shoulders sagged. That could only mean one thing—Marcus Kellman, her school-phobic student, wouldn't come into the building.

"Mr. Salinas, I'll need your help," she called.

There was no way she could handle Marcus by herself. He was a large seventh grader, who had spent his youth eating steroid-injected meat. She found Mrs. Kellman leaning against the driver's door of her beat-up Toyota sedan, waiting for the cavalry's help.

She is totally unequipped, Faye thought.

Pete joined her and they opened the back doors, attempting to coax Marcus out. The usual tactics of sweet talk, threats and fear didn't work. Growing impatient, Pete reached for Marcus.

"No!" he screamed, thrashing his arms and kicking his feet.

Pete pulled him toward the door. Attempting to help, Faye leaned into the car and grabbed his backpack just as Marcus lifted his head and spit in her face.

"Crap," she murmured, retreating from the car.

She'd been at school for less than an hour and she was ready to go home. She stormed back into the office feeling dirty.

"Faye, hold up," Marian called from her desk. "Ms. Loomis is here to see you."

Faye turned and faced an exceedingly attractive woman with white-blond hair who was standing in the lobby. She wore a gray suit and a red silk blouse accented by a string of pearls. She clutched a portfolio and an expensive leather purse.

"Hi, I'm Andi," the woman said, extending her hand.

Her eyes were cornflower blue and they radiated an intensity that commanded respect. Her high cheekbones were dusted with a light rose blush and her skin was fair, adding delicateness to her appearance. Faye felt an overwhelming desire to bow in front of her.

Faye stepped back. "You really don't want to shake my hand right now." She wondered how much spittle still hung on her chin and she plucked a tissue from the box on Marian's desk and dabbed her face.

Andi smiled slightly and pointed to her own cheek with a perfectly manicured finger. "You missed a little."

"Thanks," Faye said, completely embarrassed. "If you'll excuse me, I'll be right back. You can wait in my office. It's the first door on the left."

Andi nodded and walked past her, leaving behind a wonderful scent that wasn't heavy or offending. Faye admired her shapely derriere swaying from side to side as she floated down the corridor.

She ducked into the bathroom and quickly scrubbed her face and hands, knowing that the little bit of blush she'd applied that morning was history.

When she returned to her office, Andi's perfume filled her senses. She stood at her bookcase, clearly admiring her collection of antique books and school supplies. She held a first edition McGuffy reader in her hand, slowly turning the pages.

"This is unbelievable. Where did you get it?"

"At an antique auction. I paid fifty bucks for a whole pallet of items and that was tucked inside an old hatbox."

Andi glanced up, her eyes wide. "You're kidding."

"Nope. People clean out their relatives' attics and closets never really knowing what they've got. It winds up at auctions and scavengers like me pick it up for a song. You wouldn't believe some of the things I've found over the years."

"I'll bet. So do you sell antiques as a second career?" Andi asked, replacing the book carefully on the shelf.

"It's my hobby. I wouldn't call it a career. I have a few stalls that I rent in some buildings around town."

Andi smiled and flowed into a chair. Faye watched as she daintily crossed her legs and opened her portfolio. "Well, we should probably focus on your special education requirements, specifically the problem with Constance Richardson."

Faye flopped next to her, lacing her fingers behind her head. "Constance Richardson has absolutely no understanding of her son's needs and she's making our lives miserable. Superintendent Gleeson made it clear that you would make my troubles with her vanish."

Andi chuckled and Faye decided she had an incredible

smile. "I'm not sure that's possible. In fact, I came here today to see..." Her voice trailed off as she studied a section of her notes. "...the worst administrator to ever lead a public school in the state of Arizona. Faye Burton and her teacher Barbara Strauss are unwilling or incapable of meeting the needs of my son, Armour. For example, they refuse to allow him to participate in physical education." She gave Faye the once-over and said, "Hmm, you don't look like a bigot."

When Faye remained expressionless, Andi leaned back in the chair and rested her head against her hand. "C'mon, Ms. Burton. Can't ya take a joke?" she asked with a wink.

The mood shifted as they hugged the line between professional and personal conversation. She was drawn to Andi—a feeling she hadn't experienced in a long time.

"Is that a Texas drawl I hear?" Faye asked, deciding to cross the line.

"I try to hide it most of the time. People hear an accent and they think hick."

"I think it makes you sound interesting."

Andi stared at her and Faye felt warm all over. "Is that a fact?"

She leaned forward, her perfume wafting into Faye's personal space. It was intoxicating.

"So, Ms. Burton—"

"Please, call me Faye."

"And you can call me Andi. Look, Faye, can we speak frankly?"

"Sure. Whatever you have to say is strictly confidential. The door's closed and I'm known for keeping secrets."

Andi raised an eyebrow. "Interesting choice of words."

"What do you mean?"

Andi gazed at her notes and tapped her pen. Faye's gaze drifted to her chest, the curves of her breasts slightly straining against her tailored shirt. She quickly averted her eyes, imagining that a straight woman wouldn't appreciate being ogled.

"What do you think of Dr. Marjorie?"

Faye rolled her eyes, resisting the impulse to inform Andi that Dr. Marjorie was also known as Dr. Marshmallow. Light and fluffy with little substance. She talked expansively about the big picture but she could never give specifics.

Faye chose her words carefully. "I think she's really good at decorating a Christmas tree."

Andi laughed heartily and she slapped her knee. Only then did Faye notice that she wore no wedding band but a gold ring adorned her pinky finger.

"That's the perfect way to describe her! That woman's big hat, no cattle."

Now it was Faye's turn to laugh. "That's quite an expression."

"They're all from my granny. Now, how in the hell did Dr. Marjorie ever agree to these ridiculous demands for this kid?" She shuffled through her portfolio and withdrew A.J.'s plan. "It says here that Mom basically runs the show. We can't do anything for him without her okay. That's not ethical and I don't think it's legal."

"You're probably right. But Constance Richardson is an attorney and Dr. Marjorie is worried about a lawsuit or making the news. It's always been easier to agree to her very unreasonable demands."

"But you're thinking we need to stand up to her?"

Faye went to her file cabinet and removed a thick folder. "This is A.J.'s discipline record. Much of it's from last year when he was a sixth grader. Before then he was little and the things he did were harmless—disruptive, but harmless."

Andi flipped randomly through the referrals. "Oh, you mean like the time in third grade when he took off all his clothes and ran naked through the classroom screaming *fasty native*?"

"Yup. Harmless. And he did that last week, in addition to grabbing a boy by the hair and throwing him to the ground."

"Great," Andi said sarcastically.

She continued to skim the papers, familiarizing herself with A.J.'s many transgressions, shaking her head. "This doesn't bode well. He's getting more violent."

"And bigger," Faye added. "I'm worried that someone's going to get hurt or A.J. will accidentally hurt himself. *Then* we'll have a lawsuit."

Andi shut the folder and sighed. "Okay, now I know what

I'm dealing with. His plan comes up for review next month and we can urge an alternative placement. Maybe I can persuade her."

"What about the complaint? Do you think there's a way to stop her from going to the state and complaining about us?"

Andi shrugged. "I don't know and I don't care. Just because a parent goes to the state doesn't mean anything. I've dealt with lots of those parents and I've never lost a case yet."

Faye snorted. "I hope I'm not your first."

Andi batted her eyelashes. "Why, Ms. Burton, we Southern ladies are known for our charms. Besides this ain't my first rodeo."

Faye smiled and when Andi smiled in return, awkwardness stepped between them. It was as if she wanted to say something else because she made no effort to pick up her portfolio or the expensive purse that probably cost more than all of the purses combined that Faye had ever owned. She believed in sales and faux leather.

Finally Andi said, "Faye, I like you."

"I like you too, Andi." And she did, particularly to look at.

"Then let me tell you something. They're out to get you."

"Who?"

"Gleeson and Dr. Marjorie. Well, I think it's really just Gleeson but Dr. Marjorie's his yes woman."

"She's always been like that," Faye said. "She's a chameleon who doesn't have a mind of her own. She just agrees with the sitting superintendent to preserve her job."

"Well, you'd better start thinking along the same lines because Gleeson's looking to replace you."

Faye shrugged. "Why?"

"He says it's because of your lackluster performance but truthfully I think it's because he's certain that you're a lesbian."

She winced at Andi's word choice. She'd had her suspicions but it was difficult to hear someone else confirm them. And she knew she shouldn't be surprised. Although she'd never advertised her sexuality and she never dated co-workers, she didn't spend hundreds of dollars on makeup and clothes. It wasn't her style and to dress up would be like celebrating Halloween every day.

"Why would he think that?" she asked casually, still uncertain she could trust Andi.

"Probably because that's what Dr. Marjorie thinks."

"What?"

Andi waved her hand. "Something about running into you and your girlfriend at the mall?"

Faye wracked her brain until she remembered two Christmases ago. She'd been seeing a pediatrician who'd asked her to go shopping. They'd stopped in the Macy's cosmetics department so the woman could purchase her face cream. Dr. Marjorie saw Faye and gave her a big hug. She then spent five minutes pumping her date about their relationship. Fortunately the woman had enough sense to play coy.

"She wasn't my girlfriend," Faye said.

"But you *are* gay?"

She stared into Andi's eyes. Only her two most trusted co-workers knew about her sexuality—Jonnie Clark, the counselor, and Pete Salinas, her AP. It had taken her a year to confide in them but she had finally realized that she needed *someone* to talk to. Her second in command and the school counselor seemed like good choices.

"Yes," she answered, before she could talk herself into a lie. She held her breath, wondering if her career was about to be ruined.

"Then you need to be careful," Andi said, gathering her things and rising.

Faye knew that was true. The Glen Oaks School District was primarily upper-middle class, filled with homes that proudly displayed Republican placards during every election. She was a black sheep in an ultra-conservative area. While many of her teachers and parents may have guessed at her sexuality, she never rubbed their noses in it and never made them confront their homophobia. It was only a *little* bit of hiding she told herself. And she was comforted by the fact that in the great unlikelihood she ever gained a partner and they were ever spotted in public holding hands or kissing, she wouldn't deny it.

They walked out to Andi's car, the awkwardness returning.

Andi tossed her things into the passenger's seat and leaned against the door.

"I'm still pretty new to Phoenix and I love browsing for antiques. Any chance you'd be willing to show me the best places to shop?"

"Um, sure," Faye sputtered.

Andi's slow smile melted her and she was certain if she looked down, she'd be gone, reduced to a puddle at Andi's feet.

"Great. I'll send you an e-mail and we can make a plan."

Faye watched her drive away, realizing that she'd very much enjoyed Andi Loomis's visit, even if its purpose was to discuss Constance Richardson and her own less than propitious future. She found herself almost skipping back to the front door, excited at the prospect of seeing her socially.

"Good, you're out of your meeting," Marian said, dissolving the image of Andi. She held three phone messages in her hand. "Mrs. Cassavetes would like you to call her. Apparently Pete told her she needed to grow up after she got angry when he informed her about Jeremiah's suspension. And channel twelve called. They want to know if we're worried about our unsafe soccer goals—"

"They're unsafe?" Faye asked.

"I have no idea. But first you need to go visit Debbie McKeever in the science lab. Jasper's missing again and she's ready to call the police and file a missing persons report."

"For a tortoise?"

Marian rolled her eyes. "You know Debbie."

Faye sighed. She did indeed know Debbie, the most fiery and emotional teacher she'd ever met. Debbie loved Jasper dearly but he was known for climbing out of his habitat and wandering down the corridors.

She took the messages from Marian and headed toward the science lab, forgetting her pleasant meeting with Andi. It was back to her regularly scheduled day.

Andi kept her promise and e-mailed Faye a few hours

later, asking to see the antique stores in the valley on Saturday. They spent the day trolling through the shops of Phoenix and Glendale, including the ones where Faye had rented a stall. Andi fired questions at her about her family and hobbies but she volunteered little about her own life, except to say that she was an only child who wasn't close to her parents. They still lived in the tiny Texas town where Andi grew up and she'd spent time in Austin and Portland for her teaching career. It seemed difficult for her to talk about herself so Faye didn't press. She enjoyed Andi's company and it pleased her to think she might have a new friend.

Their last stop was Mad Hatter's Collectibles, a place where Faye had a stall. She rearranged some of the pieces and took inventory. Perched on a bookshelf in the back was something she didn't recognize, a gold unicorn.

"What the hell?"

It was about eight inches tall and the gold paint on its back had chipped away, revealing specks of white plaster. The tip of the horn was gone, leaving only a stump and robbing the poor creature of its majesty. It rested on its haunches and a square, black plastic base suggested that perhaps the intended purpose of the piece was a bookend, its mate lost.

"That's certainly interesting," Andi said, leaning over Faye's shoulder.

"I'm not sure interesting is the best word. Maybe tacky."

"If it's tacky, why did you put it up for sale?"

"I didn't. I'm guessing that someone wanted to get rid of it and just stuck it in my stall. That happens once in a while. It's like reverse shoplifting."

"Have you ever abandoned any of your stuff?" Andi asked playfully.

Faye laughed. "Only once. I had this mask that I'd gotten as part of a big lot. It was scary looking. One night I walked into the stall and some customer had moved it to the front. Scared the shit out of me. I took it to another part of the store and gave it a good home."

"How nice of you. Well, what are you going to do with this guy?"

Faye looked around. "We could probably dump him over in seventy-two. That guy can never keep track of what he has." Then an idea came to her. "On second thought I think he'd make a great gift for my sister. Her fiftieth birthday is coming up in a few months. This is perfect."

"You're kidding, right?"

"Uh, no."

"I take it there's a story there."

"The short version is simple. My sister Elise is everything I'm not—Republican, straight and rich. She's an investment banker who's married to a neurosurgeon with two perfect offspring." Faye held out the unicorn. "I believe I've found an exceptional gift for the woman who really does have everything."

Andi looked at her skeptically. "It doesn't sound like you two are close."

Faye shrugged. "We get along but we don't see each other much."

"Does she live far away?"

"If you think nine miles is far."

Andi's eyes widened. "Faye, what's that about? I would have loved to have had a sister."

"You can have mine."

"Faye!"

"Here's the thing. When our parents got divorced, Rob and I sided with our mother since it was Dad who cheated. But Elise was daddy's little girl and she went to live with him. Then she was out of the picture away at college. I've never really known her as an adult," Faye concluded. "She doesn't even know I'm gay."

"That's kinda sad."

Faye realized Andi was very close, their bodies practically touching. She turned to face her and found Andi's lips only inches away. The blue eyes bore into hers, rendering her helpless. When Andi kissed her, her arms went slack and the unicorn dropped from her hand—onto her foot.

"Shit! That hurt."

"Are you all right?" Andi asked.

"That fucker is heavy," Faye growled, rubbing her foot.

She took off her shoe and they examined the top of her foot, which wasn't broken, but a purple bruise was already forming.

"I'm sorry," Andi said. "I probably shouldn't have surprised you like that but I just couldn't help myself."

Faye shook her head. "I didn't realize…"

"That I was gay?"

"No."

Andi leaned against a wall, her hands in the back pockets of her designer jeans. She'd left an extra shirt button undone and Faye had enjoyed a clear view of her breasts and the lacy black bra she wore every time they got close.

"I usually don't set off people's gaydar. It's not that I'm hiding," she added quickly. "I really enjoy being a girl, a lipstick lesbian, I guess."

Faye grinned and picked up the unicorn. "There's nothing wrong with that. I'm all for girlie girls even though I'm not one myself."

"Great," Andi said, in a voice that sounded like an invitation.

"Does anyone at work know?"

Andi shook her head. "I keep my personal life very personal. I hope you're okay with that."

"Of course. Like I said, I keep lots of secrets," she said, arching her eyebrows.

Andi remained stoic. "I mean it, Faye. I'm incredibly closeted at work. I almost didn't move here. I can't believe there are still states where people can be fired solely based on their sexuality."

"We're not a protected class, according to the Arizona Court of Appeals—"

"Which is why I protect myself. I hope you will keep our friendship, or relationship, or whatever this is going to be, between us."

Faye nodded. "I respect your choices, Andi, especially given your position. You work with the most vulnerable of children, and in the minds of all of those who think that every gay person is also a pervert, you could be the worst kind."

"I'm glad you understand. I like a refined woman," Andi

said in her Texas drawl. She crossed the distance between them and leaned over the chair Faye was sitting in. "And since we're miles away from work, practically alone and secluded in this little shop, I want to kiss you again. Then you can peek down my shirt some more."

Faye's cheeks burned and Andi laughed before she gave Faye the best kiss of her life.

Chapter Five

The alarm on Constance's BlackBerry sounded and she rolled out from under Ira's perfect body. "I've got to get out of here," she said, silencing the alarm and rising from the hotel's exquisite king-sized bed.

He grabbed her and buried his lips in her neck. She lolled her head back, closed her eyes and savored his kisses. She could be a few minutes late to Armour's meeting. They certainly couldn't start without her and she was frequently behind schedule due to her enormous responsibilities. In fact, it was almost expected. Only this time her insatiable desire to copulate with her new boy toy would be the cause of her tardiness.

"Stay," he murmured, pulling her back under him and re-igniting their passion.

She'd known from the moment they'd shaken hands two

months ago that she wanted him. Although she'd steamrolled right over Nick Manos, who conceded everything and lost joint custody of his children, Ira had joined her for a drink. He was a smart one and he wanted to learn from the master. She'd shown him many legal tricks and as she'd suspected, he was incredibly talented in bed. It truly was quid pro quo.

She glanced at the clock and felt a little guilty. Yet as he worked his magic a sense of entitlement overwhelmed her. She rarely had this much fun at two thirty in the afternoon. She was always busy deposing a witness or reviewing a pleading. Her personal life was a joke, consisting of work and a small slice of time with Armour. She counted few people as friends and refused to associate with colleagues for fear of professional ramifications.

She gazed into his soft brown eyes and a single tear rolled down her cheek. How could she feel so alone when she was cocooned in bed with a wonderful man?

"Hey, don't go there," he whispered. "The rest of the world isn't here. Let me take you somewhere you want to be."

She closed her eyes and let him lead her away.

"I'm so sorry."

Constance swept into the conference room, twenty minutes late. Melanie had called to warn them but from the cold stares she received, she could tell they didn't care. They all thought they had important jobs but really they were just underpaid civil servants who could be easily manipulated. She certainly knew that from her past experience with Glen Oaks. Every one of her demands had always been met and today would be no different. She was on her game. Maybe a little afternoon delight was a great stimulator.

"Not a problem, Constance. They just called Armour down to join us," Andrea Loomis said with a tight smile. "I think you know everyone except Dale Nowicki, the new psychologist here at Cedar Hills."

She nodded at Nowicki, a middle-aged, chubby man with

a ponytail and a goatee. He wore a Hawaiian shirt and tan corduroy pants, obviously an incompetent or Loomis wouldn't bother to be present at a routine meeting. She glanced around the table at the rest of the usual players—Faye Burton, Barbara Strauss and the young technology teacher, Ms. Rasmussen. Technology and art were the only regular classes that Armour attended. He was fascinated by computers, which looked very similar to his beloved television. And with Ms. Rasmussen's help, he stayed focused and did exactly what she said—most of the time.

The door swung open and Armour bounded in. "Mommy!" he cried when he saw her.

He ran into her arms and she steeled herself for his hug, wondering what part of his lunch would inevitably transfer from his dirty shirt onto her Donna Karan silk blouse. All of those judgmental eyes were on her and she knew what was expected. They thought she was a horrible parent who didn't have a clue about her son or his needs. She'd show them. She squeezed him tightly and then pulled back, careful not to look down at her blouse immediately.

"How are you, sweetheart. Are you having a good day?"

"Uh-huh. I'm so glad you're here."

She knew he meant it with the greatest sincerity. She pointed to the empty chair next to her and he plopped down in it. She glanced down at her shirt and noticed a tiny dot of mustard next to her middle button. *Fabulous.*

From across the room Loomis opened a file and put on her reading glasses. "Okay, this is a yearly review of A.J.'s Individualized Educational Plan to analyze his progress toward his goals and discuss the next steps." She turned to Strauss. "Barbara, would you like to go first? How's he doing?"

Strauss cleared her throat. "Well, A.J. has his good days and his bad days." She glanced at him and smiled warmly. "It's very hard to know which day is which since a good day can devolve quickly if there's something that triggers his emotions. I know everyone remembers the day he grabbed Victoria's hair, and more recently we've had incidences where he's destroyed other students' work, hit a student in the face with a book, which did require medical attention, and last week he decided to jump off his desk like Superman, but he fell against another child's desk on his way down. Fortunately he only sustained a bruise to his cheek but it was pretty close to his eye."

"It really hurt," Armour blurted, tapping at his face.

Most of the purpling had vanished but a dark half-moon still marred his little cheek. Constance bore her gaze into Strauss determined to move the meeting along at breakneck pace. She knew what they wanted and time was money.

"I still don't understand how this happened. I don't believe Mrs. Strauss or Ms. Burton ever clarified how Armour managed to climb on a desk without anyone stopping him. Were you in the room, Mrs. Strauss?"

The smile vanished from Strauss's face. "As I told you over the phone, Ms. Richardson, I was present but I had my back to A.J. since I was helping another student. He had very clear instructions to remain in his seat and do his work." She paused and took a breath. "This is the problem, and frankly this is the piece of his plan that needs to be reviewed. If a child cannot sit quietly and work independently for a few minutes without endangering himself or others, then I have serious doubts about his placement in a public school setting. He needs a different environment."

"That's not going to happen," she said specifically to Loomis. "Armour will not lose his place at Cedar Hills merely because Mrs. Strauss cannot control her class, or," she quickly added before Strauss interrupted, "because she needs more help. What are the chances of getting her an aide?"

Loomis shook her head. "I wish that were an option but the district has allocated all of its funds for the year and there's no money for another aide."

"That's not my problem. Perhaps once the state reviews my complaint they will see fit to order Glen Oaks to provide more assistance."

"Does that mean you've submitted the complaint?" Loomis asked pointedly.

"It's completed and sitting on my desk." Her gaze shifted to Burton. "I was waiting to see the outcome of this meeting."

Burton looked up from her notes and glanced at the special education director before turning to Constance. "You have to understand that an aide won't solve these issues. When A.J. blows everything happens very fast. It wouldn't matter if someone was sitting right next to him. That person couldn't stop him from jumping out of his seat and running around the room. When he hit that little girl in the face with the book it took less than a second. No one is going to respond that quickly unless they're standing over him like a football player ready for the snap."

"Football," Armour said with a wide grin. "Fasty native!"

The room went quiet until he resettled himself with a crayon and a piece of a paper that Rasmussen set before him. He started humming the theme to *Mr. Zex.*

Loomis held up her hands. "Ms. Richardson, we could certainly look at that option—"

"An aide won't help, Andi," Burton interrupted sharply. She stared at Constance. "Perhaps you *should* file your complaint. I have confidence that once the state peruses A.J.'s disciplinary record, they'll side with the school."

Loomis touched her arm. "Faye—"

"Do you agree, Director Loomis?" Constance asked. "Should I file my complaint?"

Loomis sighed, obviously sensing she was losing control. "Let's set that issue to the side," Loomis said, offering Burton a hard stare.

An odd look passed between them. When Burton held up a hand in acquiescence, Loomis continued. "Why don't we ask Ms. Rasmussen to share her observations about technology class and I'd still like Mrs. Strauss to discuss A.J.'s progress toward his goals."

She shifted her gaze to pretty Ms. Rasmussen but her mind was still focused on the exchange between Loomis and Burton. There was something there—something inappropriate. Burton's tone and the look bordered on insubordination, and while she didn't think Andrea Loomis was Faye Burton's superior, it was still unprofessional and certainly unplanned. She'd let her guard down and snapped at a colleague in front of a parent. Perhaps Burton really didn't care much for the director—or perhaps she did. Constance had heard rumors about her sexuality ever since Armour had arrived at Cedar Hills. Many of the parents mentioned it as juicy gossip, a tidbit of information to offer at a cocktail party that made them seem powerful. Honestly she didn't care but she knew Arizona statute well enough to know that a gay principal would want to keep her sexuality private, particularly in a district like Glen Oaks.

Rasmussen finished and Strauss picked up immediately, reading from her notes. Constance glanced at Burton but her eyes settled on Loomis, who listened intently to Strauss's babble. She never would have labeled the woman a lesbian. Even her short hair was chic, not butch. Her attire was enviable and Constance once had inquired about a particular designer when Loomis had donned a stylish over-jacket. She'd heard about lesbians who looked like movie stars and one of her friends in L.A. had gossiped about several actresses who Constance never would've guessed were gay or bi. It was their way of hiding.

Could Director Loomis and Principal Burton possibly be a couple? There were certainly ways to find out.

She nodded appropriately as Strauss finished. She'd heard enough to participate in the discussion. If lawyers were good at anything it was listening to a conversation while thinking of something else at the same time.

After outlining Armour's plan they returned to the issue of environment. She was adamant that he remain at Cedar Hills but she wanted to hear their ideas since they clearly had an agenda.

"Not that I would ever seriously consider it, but where would he go if he wasn't here?" she asked.

Loomis answered. "We'd send him to private placement, most likely Arizona Behavioral Health. They have a great program for students like A.J. Small classes with a behavior management piece. It would be perfect."

"For all of *you*, yes," she said. "Wouldn't you just love to get rid of him?"

Burton swiveled her chair to face her. "How dare you suggest that competent educators would simply write off a child or push him out? We are trying to do what is best for him in this situation. His needs have changed and Cedar Hills is no longer the appropriate place for him. His behaviors are becoming more severe and there's another issue we haven't mentioned yet. A.J. is getting physically larger and stronger, which means his hormones are changing as well. Mrs. Strauss has noticed him taking an interest in females and that's entirely natural. Unfortunately, I fear we're on a collision course. He's entering the teenage maturation process without the normal ability to adapt. He will most likely harm himself or someone else if he is allowed to remain in a public school setting."

Burton settled back in her chair and Constance remained frozen, certain she gave away nothing, although a thread of fear worked its way deep inside her heart. She was certainly aware of what would happen if he ever hurt anyone and the civil and criminal complications she would face. Yet she would never show that fear to these people.

"I guess that will be a matter for the state to decide. I'd hoped that this meeting would sway me to drop my complaint with the state but it's done just the opposite. I'm more convinced than ever that you all would like to get rid of Armour."

Strauss sighed. "Ms. Richardson, I love A.J. He's a wonderful child but he's changing."

Strauss insisted on reiterating everything Burton had already covered and Constance was bored, thinking again about how much educators loved to hear themselves talk unaware of the ticking clock and the taxpayer money flying down the garbage disposal. She calculated that this meeting was costing a few thousand dollars, particularly because both Loomis and Burton were present.

She knew they couldn't change his placement without her consent. She glanced again at Andrea Loomis, fascinated by the idea that someone with such incredible fashion sense could be a lesbian. A few surveillance shots from Caliente Investigations would satisfy her curiosity and possibly give her some leverage with Burton and Cedar Hills. She doubted they could force her hand but it never hurt to have bargaining power.

Chapter Six

Faye cleared the confiscated candy, stink bombs and poppers from her desk drawer by tossing it all into her garbage can. "I hate Halloween," she muttered, erasing the memory of the last week for another year.

The children had either consumed or had confiscated every piece of detritus that remained from the most ridiculous holiday she could imagine. She knew it was against the gay code to hate Halloween but most of her gay friends didn't spend an entire week policing the colored hair, ridiculous costumes and bags of candy that wandered onto campus. Her lesbian credentials were still in order—at least she loved cats.

Her phone rang, as if it could sense she was paused from her work. She glanced at the display and smiled.

"Hey, Texas."

"Hey, I'm gonna miss dinner. You're on your own." Andi

sounded pissed and rushed. "What's wrong?"

She sighed and Faye could hear her office door click shut. "*Our* boss decided I should present in front of the school board tonight. They want to know about the enrollment figures. *Tonight.* I'm on my way to a school visit and I've got three meetings back-to-back afterward. When in the hell am I going to have time to create a flippin' PowerPoint?" she said, a trace of her Southern accent slipping out. "Not to mention the fact that I am totally underdressed for a presentation."

Faye chuckled softly, remembering how beautiful she'd looked in the striking plum blouse and tailored gray slacks she'd chosen that morning. "I may be biased but I thought you looked great when you left."

"You are biased and you're not a femme. I have three rules: never sleep with a woman on the first date, run like crazy from any lover with a concealed weapons permit and always wear a power suit for a presentation."

"Can you go home and change?"

"Maybe." Another long sigh. "Look, I gotta go. Maybe we could get together tomorrow?"

Faye scrolled through her e-mail, only half listening.

"Babe, are you with me?" Andi scolded. "Are you answering your e-mail? I can hear you smackin' those keys."

Caught. She pushed her chair away from the desk and focused. "Okay, okay. I have to go to the board meeting too. Barbara Strauss is receiving the Teacher of the Month award."

"Shit. That's right. I can't believe I forgot about Barbara."

"By the way Gleeson called today. He wanted to know how A.J.'s doing. Do you know anything about that?"

"Uh-huh," was Andi's reply.

She grinned. "Now who's distracted?"

"Sorry. I'm just throwing a few of those slides together. I meant to call you earlier and give you a heads-up. One of my meetings today is with Gleeson, Dr. Marjorie and Constance Richardson. She still wants him in P.E. She didn't like that we stood up to her so she's demanding an audience with the superintendent to explain her position. She's using that state complaint as leverage."

"And the Glen Oaks School District is happy to oblige," Faye concluded.

Andi chuckled. "You got it."

"Texas, do I need to worry about this?"

"No, I don't think so. I'll handle it, babe."

Faye smiled, reassured. Andi was amazing at her job and she totally trusted her.

"Look, I'll see you tonight. Maybe we could grab takeout and go back to my place?"

"Well, that's one idea," Faye said slowly. "You know, we've gone to your place the last few times. I'd really like to spend some time with Unlucky."

"He's a cat, Faye. He's independent. And you know how hard it is for me to go mobile. Besides," she added, "you want your girl to look pretty, don't you?"

She grinned. Going mobile was Andi's expression for the incredible task it was to cart all of her necessities to Faye's place whenever they stayed there, particularly on a work night.

"You are one fine-looking woman. Okay, I'll stop by the house before the board meeting and feed him."

"Thanks, babe," she said in a breathy voice that told Faye she would be rewarded in bed that night for her continued sacrifice. "I'll see you later."

She dropped the handset onto the cradle and stared at the phone. Andi had her three rules but she only had one: Don't get involved with people in your school district. And she'd broken it for Andi.

The governing board room was nearly full by the time Faye arrived for the meeting. Someone touched her arm and she turned and greeted Jonnie Clark.

"Hey, are you here for Barbara?"

Jonnie nodded and Faye felt someone tap her on the shoulder. "Hello, Faye."

Jonnie motioned toward two empty chairs and Faye faced the familiar voice—Karl Horner, a member of the board, and a man she was rather sure knew she was gay and had a problem with it.

He set his hands on his hips and looked around the room. "I understand we're honoring Barbara Strauss tonight."

She nodded. "Yes, she's very worthy. She's one of the best special education teachers I've ever met."

He leaned closer and she could smell his pungent aftershave. "She's got the Richardson boy, doesn't she?"

She knew that Constance regularly e-mailed the superintendent and the board with her complaints about Barbara's inability to meet A.J.'s needs.

"Yes, A.J. keeps her on her toes," she said, unwilling to gossip or share details about school matters with board members.

"I'd just hate to get into a legal tussle with her."

Faye knew Karl had been the victim of the Steamroller when he divorced his second wife. "She's a piranha, Faye. We need to do whatever we can to keep her happy. I've told Bill Gleeson and Andrea Loomis the same thing."

She nodded automatically, recognizing the meaning behind his words.

She congratulated Barbara and took the seat next to Jonnie. Andi worked at the front with the computer technician to prepare her presentation. She had apparently run home and changed into a smart black suit and when she bent over to pick up her briefcase, Faye's breath caught at the sight of her shapely bottom.

"She looks great. See something you like?" Jonnie teased.

Jonnie was the one person who knew she was dating Andi. "Can you blame me?"

"No, not really," Jonnie replied.

She was momentarily speechless. She'd never heard Jonnie make a flirtatious comment about a woman.

"Will you please rise for the Pledge of Allegiance?" the board president requested.

The meeting began and Gleeson immediately launched into the Teacher of the Month award. After Barbara accepted her plaque, most everyone left but she stuck around through the remainder of the meeting and Andi's presentation, which despite the last-minute notice, was incredibly insightful and detailed. She expected nothing less from her.

Andi was an eloquent public speaker and Faye always enjoyed watching and listening to her. She was exceptionally poised and she gestured with purpose. Her voice had a pleasant lilt that conveyed confidence with only a slight trace of the Texas drawl that revealed her roots. Watching her explain the figures and conclusions to the attentive five board members, she could tell they were impressed.

And it didn't hurt that she was beautiful. Although she wore her hair short, few would ever guess that the woman in the Prada shoes with the expensive manicure was a lesbian. Her stylish outfits were the envy of straight women, who often complimented her on her fashion sense. She knew Andi's appearance was her choice, borne of what she loved, but Faye wondered if it also served as a cloak to hide her sexuality. It was a concern she hadn't mentioned to her.

They asked her a few questions, thanked her for the information and dismissed her. Faye caught her eye and winked and she smiled slightly as she returned to her seat across the room. The rest of the business items were quickly resolved with little discussion. After the gavel sounded the adjournment, she headed for the exit and Andi followed.

She waited for her by the elevator and both of them glanced back at the boardroom. They were alone for the moment.

"Nice job, Texas."

"Thanks. I can't stand Gleeson. Have I told you that?"

"Yeah, I think we're in agreement there." She lovingly tucked a wisp of her hair behind her ear. "So, what'll it be? Thai or Mexican?"

"Thai, just nothing too spicy."

"I'll meet you at your place."

"Faye?"

"Yeah, babe?"

"You're the best."

She laughed. "You're just saying that because I agreed to stay at your condo tonight."

"Well, that's not the only reason but I am glad we're going

there," she admitted. "Your house is so small."

"My house is *historic*. It's quaint and charming."

"It is definitely charming. It's just that right now I want to eat and relax, and then I want to take you to bed."

Faye caressed her cheek and was about to step away, when a sound immediately caught her attention and she knew they weren't alone. They both whipped their heads toward the boardroom door. Dr. Marjorie stood in the hallway, holding a pile of folders in her arms, trying to balance them and her purse. In the second that it took all of them to acknowledge each other's presence, Faye knew that Marjorie hadn't just emerged from the boardroom or the door would still be closing. Obviously she'd exited through the side door and come around the corner, stopping when she saw the two of them together.

Faye realized she was standing in Andi's personal space and she was certain she wore the same goofy expression she always did when they were alone. *And if Marjorie saw me play with her hair and touch her cheek...*

"Do you need help, Marjorie?" Andi asked, already advancing to her and taking some of the folders.

Faye disappeared out the front while Andi and Marjorie redistributed the load. Andi would be panicked. Faye had learned that Andi's fear of being outed lived at the edge of her brain and affected every decision she made. Whenever people began discussing their personal lives, she either changed the subject or remained silent while the straight people around her proclaimed the virtues of their spouses. She wouldn't go to any public place within a five-mile radius of the school district boundaries and Faye was under strict orders never to be affectionate unless Andi was positive they were alone.

It was a policy Faye accepted because the situation was perfect. Like Faye, Andi avoided commitment, having been burned in the past—at least that's what she claimed. Faye wondered if her hesitation derived from their close working relationship. If they didn't work together would Andi want more? And how would she feel about that?

She climbed in her truck and sighed. It was going to be a long evening. She quickly punched in Rob's number but got his voice mail. "Hey, bro. Hope your life is good. Sorry that it didn't work out with Sau but maybe now you could find a real woman to date. I found a gift for Elise and I can't wait for you to see it."

"I'm sure she knows," Andi said for the eighth time.

"Maybe not. We don't know what she saw," Faye argued. "She was carrying all of that stuff. Her mind was probably somewhere else. You know how it is when you're thinking of one thing and then you see something. It takes time for your brain to adjust."

Andi threw the empty takeout containers in the trash and crossed her arms. "Honey, do you really believe that hooey you're slingin'?"

She took a deep breath. They'd had this conversation for almost an hour and she felt like she was on a merry-go-round. She'd tried to calm Andi with every persuasive technique she could imagine—logic, emotional appeal and even a little anger. She was back to logic. "Honey, what's done is done. There's nothing we can do about it tonight. I really want you to tell me about the meeting with Constance Richardson."

Andi rubbed her temples and Faye thought she might be making progress. "Okay, I'll get off this," she conceded, "but I want to say one more thing. Just so we're clear."

"Fine."

"We live in gay hell. I hope you know that. This is nothing like Austin or Portland. This is Arizona and both of us could be reprimanded, get letters in our file and be fired. And it would probably be worse for you because you're the one with direct contact, the one who is supposedly molding and shaping young minds."

"Obviously into the shape of a vagina."

"That's not funny," she said, trying not to laugh. "This place is hell," she said again.

It was the moment to drop the topic but Faye couldn't. "Then why are you here, babe? I'm incredibly thrilled that you moved to the desert but if Phoenix is so awful, why'd you come here?"

Andi grabbed a dishrag from the sink and wiped the counters. They'd been together for a few months, long enough for Faye to learn her diversionary tactics, one of which was cleaning up. The minute she reached for the dishes or opened cabinets to put things away, Faye had realized she was inclined to help and the physical activity naturally changed the subject. She'd lost count of the times Andi had dodged a conversation.

She bit her lip and thought about what she wanted. Tonight was not the night to hold a mirror in front of Andi's flaws. She swept her up and kissed her neck. "I'm sorry if I made it tough for you tonight. I never should have touched you and I promise from now on I'll keep my hands to myself."

Andi moaned slightly as Faye's hands burrowed underneath her UT Austin T-shirt and cupped her breasts.

"Only in public," she corrected, her voice ragged with desire. "When we're alone you can have whatever you want."

Faye stepped away and smiled. "Whatever I want? I want you to tell me about this meeting. *Then* we'll play some adult games."

"Hey!"

"Honey, this is on my mind. You need to tell me what happened."

She groaned. "Fine."

Once they'd poured some red wine and curled up on the couch, Andi recounted the meeting.

"To summarize quickly, she was condescending, arrogant and downright threatening. Now can we go to bed?"

Faye grinned. "And you're going to kowtow to every one of her demands, right?"

"Hell, no! That woman's two sandwiches short of a picnic if she thinks she can just steamroll over me."

She loved it when Andi got upset because she'd inject all of her grandmother's old sayings into the conversation and her drawl was thick. "So what does she want?"

"She wants A.J. in more regular classes. If that happens I'm sure she'll drop the complaint."

Her jaw dropped. "You're kidding."

She shook her head. "She thinks he's perfectly capable of attending a regular P.E. class with the other children and the school is failing to place him in the least restrictive environment."

"That's the dumbest thing I've ever heard. It's bad enough in art and he can't keep his clothes on in Barb's room. Can you see him in Donna Fleming's general P.E. class? He'd probably whack somebody in the head with a bat." She looked at her and took a deep breath. "Please tell me you've got a plan."

"I think it's a ploy. Constance knows you want him out of Cedar Hills so she's going to push in the opposite direction—"

"In the hopes that the status quo is maintained and he doesn't go anywhere."

She nodded and raised her wineglass. "Exactly."

"Will it work?"

She shrugged. "Hard to say. Gleeson and Marjorie listened and pacified her. After she left they asked me for my opinion and I told them. I'm not sure what they'll do but don't be surprised if Marjorie directs you to give him a P.E. class."

"Please, no," Faye moaned.

"Honestly I think something drastic would have to happen for a placement change to occur."

"Taking off his clothes in front of the other children wasn't drastic enough?"

"It's a special ed class, babe. How many phone calls did you get from irate parents?"

Andi had asked a rhetorical question and knew it. There were no complaints because special education parents were incredibly sensitive to other children. They would never point a finger at a child with a disability and demand some sort of disciplinary action, knowing that someday the finger could be pointed at their own kid.

"I really hope you're wrong, Texas. If something major has to happen for us to move him, then it probably means another child's going to get hurt."

"The law's a screwy thing. Now I've had enough of this school talk. Like you said, there's nothing we can do tonight about what Marjorie saw or Constance Richardson wants. But I know what *I* want."

She rose from the couch and stood over her. Faye gazed up at her fabulous body as she pulled the T-shirt over her head. Faye rested her cheek against Andi's smooth belly and stroked her buttocks, thinking back to the moment she'd bent over during the board meeting.

"Well," she drawled. "Are you gonna make a move or am I gonna keep these britches on forever?"

Chapter Seven

The Muzak version of "Deck the Halls" filled the elevator and Constance Richardson rolled her eyes. It was only the Tuesday after Thanksgiving and already Christmas was everywhere. She expected the malls to be decorated with ribbons and trimming, as Thanksgiving was like firing a starting pistol, a signal for the ridiculous consumerism to begin. But she was appalled when she'd entered her office building the following Monday to find an enormous silver Christmas tree in the lobby and the reception desk draped in garland. It seemed little elves had spent the weekend transforming the glass high-rise into a tacky Santa's workshop.

Her cell phone rang as she exited the elevator. *Ira*. She waited until she was cloistered in the privacy of her own office before she answered.

"What?"

He exhaled deeply. "Is that any way to greet the man who's taking you skiing over Christmas?"

She scowled. "What the hell are you talking about?"

"Well, I thought about surprising you on Christmas Eve but then I realized that you'd probably need some time to make arrangements for A.J."

"His name's Armour," she corrected. "And you're crazy if you think we're going anywhere together over the holidays."

"Why is that so crazy? And I like A.J. a lot better. It suits him."

She raised an eyebrow. "Oh, really?"

She dropped her briefcase on her desk and prepared for a fight. He was an idiot—an incredibly beautiful idiot in bed—but an idiot, nonetheless.

"Ira, let me be clear. We're not taking any vacations together. Our relationship is strictly sexual. Let me use the language of your generation since nearly *a decade and a half* separates us. We're fuck buddies, friendly fucks, friends with benefits. All of those adequately describe our situation." She was on a roll now. "And if you think that I could leave Armour with any random individual, you're crazy. He's an autistic child who cannot handle change. I have no friends or family who will help me. I'm alone. That would mean I'd have to hire a professional service, a stranger. And while we slalomed down the slopes or got cozy by the fireplace, he'd be screaming like a maniac for days. Then we'd return and I'd pay the price for another week, trying to calm him down. So your proposal is ridiculous."

She paused, waiting for him to respond, but he said nothing. She swallowed hard, her anxiety growing. What if he hung up? What if he never called her again? She realized her hands were shaking and it almost sounded audible in the unbearable silence. She'd gone too far.

"Ira?" she whispered, in a manner that was foreign to her. She sounded weak, unsure. She hated that tone and fortunately it rarely escaped from the deep recesses of her heart and gave itself voice.

He cleared his throat and said, "Thank you for clarifying

our situation. I'll let you know the next time I need a quick fuck." He disconnected.

She slammed the receiver down, rage consuming her anxiety. How dare he speak to her like that?

A neon yellow sticky note posted on the base of her PDA stand caught her attention. *Armour to Santa.* She'd written the note because she couldn't remember that, although her son was using deodorant, he still demanded to see Santa Claus, unable to let go of the idea that a rotund man dressed in red velvet slipped into his house and brought him presents.

Her mind flipped to the previous year. They had been at home on Cathy's day off. She had been working in her office while he sat in front of the T.V., mesmerized by that ridiculous cartoon, *Mr. Zex.* It was his favorite program and he insisted on singing the theme song constantly. A commercial came on and when she heard the familiar, "HO, HO, HO," she knew what would happen next.

He quickly appeared at her door. "Santa! Take me to Santa!"

"Armour, we've already been three times. Santa knows what you want."

He'd stormed through the condo, hurling open the balcony door and hanging over the railing twelve stories above the ground. Her stomach plummeted and she rushed outside. She had no idea that he'd figured out how to work the special lock she'd installed.

"Come back inside, Armour. You know you're not supposed to be out here."

"I want to see Santa."

"We'll talk about it inside. Come on." She worked for her most soothing voice, attempting to hide her panic and frustration.

He coughed and then spit over the railing. "Ha! Ha!"

He turned toward her, the front of his IZOD shirt covered in mucous. She was revolted and for a second—only a second—she imagined rushing forward and pushing him over the railing. It would happen so fast that his expression would never change. She'd never see the pain or betrayal in his eyes since he processed events slowly. She knew she could get away with it. He was an unpredictable child who was difficult to manage and had a history of tricking her and coming out on the balcony. More than a few people had complained to the front desk about his propensity to spit from the twelfth floor. Her life would be her own again. She could free herself of this tortuous burden. It would be so easy.

She looked up and saw him gazing into her eyes. He looked wise and a small grin crossed his face, as if he could read her mind. She took a step to pull him away but he jumped back and spun in a circle. When he stopped he pointed a finger at her and laughed.

"Fasty native!"

She shook her head and guided him back inside and relocked the door. She'd never discerned what he meant when he uttered the phrase but she'd heard it a million times.

He was a mystery. Ira was a mystery. It must be a male thing. She made a note to send Ira an expensive bottle of scotch as a peace offering. She would never apologize but he'd get the hint.

She glanced through the small pile of mail that sat in her in basket. Two things interested her: a large manila envelope from Caliente Investigators and a letter from the department of education.

She ripped open the answer to her complaint. She scanned the three pages, a smile working its way across her lips. The state was sending a representative to investigate Cedar Hills. No doubt such a visit would devour much of Andrea Loomis's time as she prepared whatever paperwork and files the state demanded to see and then she would need to be personally available to meet with the representative when he or she arrived. Constance imagined Bill Gleeson and Marjorie Machabell would be greatly annoyed that their special education director would be consumed by the whims of a single parent and a frivolous complaint. And Constance knew her complaint would lead nowhere. Any gains that could be achieved for Armour would be at Marjorie's direction. Perhaps the state would advise the district to comply but Constance knew her position was greatly compromised by a single factor—Armour.

He was a danger and she knew it. She went to the window and looked out at her magnificent view, her anxiety scraping against her brain. She'd never acknowledge publicly that there was any truth to Faye Burton's concerns. She knew enough school law to know that most of the worries never transformed into real problems. Very rarely was there a school shooting, bus accident or teacher misconduct, but because of the media's coverage and sensationalism, the public thought awful things happened at schools every day. But they didn't because the truth was simple—teachers were good at their jobs. She knew this. She knew that Barbara Strauss was an exceptional educator and that was the point. Armour was entitled to such a wonderful teacher. *Cora's son* was entitled to such a wonderful situation as Cedar Hills. She loved the school but she'd have to fight against them to keep him there. It was quid pro quo.

She returned to her desk and set the letter aside. She reached for the large manila envelope from Caliente Investigations. "They are just so good," she murmured, withdrawing the stack of eight-by-ten photos. She frowned slightly, disappointed that Ms. Loomis and Ms. Burton didn't provide nearly as many incriminating moments as Nick Manos. Most of the pictures were of them shopping or walking. Never did they hold hands or kiss. However, there were two pictures where the photographer had caught them in an intimate moment in a public place. One showed Loomis obviously getting ready to leave while Burton leaned against her car and touched her shoulder. The women looked lovingly at each other. The other photo was caught from behind at just the right moment when Burton was pulling Loomis toward her and whispering in her ear.

She placed the photos back in the envelope and locked them away in her credenza. They were her security policy and she might never need to use them, although a little part of her, the part that loved confrontation and takedown, hoped she'd get to bury Andrea Loomis and Faye Burton.

Chapter Eight

Pandy's gaze drifted to the clock above Ms. Clark's desk. Two forty-five. In fifteen minutes the dismissal bell would start Christmas break. Although she loved her group sessions with the other gay kids, her mind was focused on two weeks of freedom. And that meant a chance to visit with Mama and her new family, which included a stepfather named Joe and twin half sisters Shelby and Ciara.

Pandy had only seen a picture of them, one that her mother had sent to her in a birthday card five months ago. She carried the photo in her wallet and before she went to sleep, she'd stare at it, smiling with hope. It showed the four of them together, and although she'd never met Joe, he looked kind, nothing like the men who had frequented their house in Salt Lake—especially Uncle Lemont.

She couldn't recall his face, only his hands. When Mama had brought him home, she'd automatically tacked the word uncle onto the introduction as she did every time a new guy entered her life. Pandy never understood why. They were all losers but she'd never forget Lemont's long, bony fingers reaching across the couch to touch her knee while they watched TV He'd set his hand down while Mama was distracted and Pandy's gaze would shift from the TV set to those fingers wrapped around her kneecap. His hands were never clean even after he washed them. He was a mechanic like her father and Mama had said something about them knowing each other. He had big gold rings on three of his fingers and she'd heard him brag to Mama that those rings were his fighting trademark. Any man that got in a fight with Lemont always got branded by his rings.

Fortunately Lemont didn't last long. Mama caught him with his hand on Pandy's knee and threatened to tell the cops if he didn't get out. He left right away but Pandy thought Mama was lucky that she didn't get branded.

She shuddered as the memory faded and when she looked up, Ms. Clark was staring at her.

"I can see that everyone is a little distracted since we're about to go on winter break. Is anyone doing anything special?"

"I'm going to see my mother," Pandy said meekly. She rarely volunteered in group and Ms. Clark often had to prod her to participate. She readily shared things when they met alone but she would never mention her secrets to a group of gossipy eighth graders. She couldn't understand why she'd brought it up but saying it out loud to others made it important.

Ms. Clark smiled. Pandy had already told her about the visit but she could tell Ms. Clark was pleased that she'd mentioned it.

"Pandy, that's right. What are you guys going to do together?"

She shrugged. She really had no idea. Mama had told her that they'd all go to dinner but that the family couldn't commit to anything else since they might take Shelby and Ciara to Disneyland. But Pandy hoped that she and Mama could go shopping or out to lunch while Joe watched the kids. She pictured them sitting on a bench at the mall, drinking coffee and people-watching.

Ms. Clark smiled. "I'm sure you'll have a great time. When was the last time you saw your mother?"

"About two and a half years ago."

From the look on her face, Pandy guessed that Ms. Clark didn't approve. What kind of mother would refuse to see her child for over two years? But Pandy knew why. Her mother had explained everything to her in a letter. She was trying to get her life together. She'd met Joe. She was in AA and she wanted a new beginning with her new family. Pandy was a reminder of their awful past. Initially she'd been angry until she thought back to her life in Salt Lake and her own images of the bad times. She decided she had no right to begrudge her mother a fresh start. After all, Mama gave her a new life—at least the state of Utah had.

While another student shared his plans for break, Pandy doodled in her sketchbook that always sat open on her lap during group. She drew a hill with trees and a row of ten headstones, all bearing her name. When the bell rang, she rushed to pack up but Ms. Clark stopped her.

"Pandy, could you hang out and talk for just a sec?"

"Sure."

After the other students left Ms. Clark joined her on the sofa. "First, I've got some amazing news for you. The leadership team picked your mural design for the amphitheater. Isn't that terrific?"

Shocked, Pandy grinned. She couldn't believe it. Ms. Taylor, the art teacher, had encouraged her to submit her design to the committee and she had wanted to please Ms. Taylor, who seemed to think it was something special.

"I thought about announcing it in group but I realized you might be embarrassed. But I don't think you have anything to be embarrassed about," she added. "It's an incredible idea."

She shrugged. "Thanks for telling me."

"Are you nervous about seeing your mom? I mean it's been a long time."

"Yeah, I know."

"Well, don't get me wrong, I'm glad she's coming to visit. I also know that sometimes these meetings are hard for a lot of reasons. People have different expectations and it doesn't always go how we think it will."

She said nothing. She knew Ms. Clark didn't want her to get her hopes up about the meeting. Her mother usually disappointed her—promises of visits that never occurred and offers to come home that were suddenly withdrawn. Once she'd even suggested that someday Pandy could rejoin the family. But the next time they talked Mama explained that she'd fallen off the wagon and been drunk when she said it. Pandy understood. And she was certain it would be different this time.

Ms. Clark went to her desk and grabbed her silly sunflower pen. "I'm going to give you my cell number, okay? If you feel like you need to talk over the break, you can call me. Don't worry about bothering me. You won't."

She nodded and stuffed the business card in her bag. Ms. Clark gave her a big hug and then she headed for the parking lot. She wouldn't need to call Ms. Clark. She was sure of it.

Grandpa drummed his fingers on the steering wheel outside the Hometown Buffet while they listened to some old Christmas carols on the radio. He glanced at his watch and sighed. "She's late. She was always late to school," he muttered.

Pandy shifted in her seat and looked at her reflection in the side view mirror. She'd put some barrettes in her chopped brown hair and removed her customary black eyeliner. Typically she was described as a Goth but for this meeting with her mother she'd decided on a collared blouse and a clean pair of jeans. Another glance in the mirror and she was satisfied. Mama wouldn't be scared of her own daughter.

Hurried shoppers bustled out of the mall with numerous packages. It was three days before Christmas and panic was written across their faces. Their cell phones were glued to their ears and she heard a young couple arguing as they got into their car. Amid all of the chaos she watched a mother emerge from the Hometown Buffet holding a little girl. She was about two and dressed in a gray sweat suit. She held out her hand and motioned to a snowman painted on the glass window. The mother bounced her against her hip and let her touch the paint, which ignited peals of squeaky laughter from the child. The mother pointed to the snowman's eyes, ears and carrot nose, and Pandy imagined she was asking her to name the parts of the snowman's body.

Pandy smiled. What a wonderful mother she must be. Then the woman turned around and Pandy's jaw dropped. It was *her* mother. The stringy blond hair that Pandy remembered was styled into a cute short cut and she was definitely thinner.

"Aw, Christ," Grandpa growled. "Well, you better go."

"Aren't you coming in?"

Grandpa shook his head and fiddled with the radio. "I got nothing to say to her. Call me when you're done and I'll come get you."

She slid out of the car and headed toward her mother, who recognized her in a second.

"Hi, baby. It's good to see you."

Mama embraced her and she almost cried. They stood together until she felt a tug on her hair.

"Hey, come on, Shelby," Mama said, laughing. "Pandy, this is your half sister, Shelby."

She smiled at the beautiful little girl who had her mother's blue eyes, just like Pandy. "Hi, Shelby." She held out her index finger and let Shelby grasp it tightly.

"Well, we better get inside. Where's Pop?"

"He's not coming."

Mama frowned and shook her head. "Why would I expect anything to change?"

They went inside and she met Joe, a handsome man who reminded her of Patrick Dempsey. He asked her lots of questions about school and she told them all about how much she liked sketching and being a student mentor. Often she repeated things because it was hard to have a conversation in the noisy restaurant filled with families taking advantage of the cheap food.

"I found out today that I won an award," she offered, hoping that she didn't sound stuck up. She wanted Mama to be proud of her and then perhaps she'd want them to spend more time together.

Joe and Mama smiled. "What kind of an award?" he asked.

"Well, it's not really an award, I guess. It's more like an honor. I drew this picture and the school chose it to be a mural on our new amphitheater. It's kinda cool."

They smiled at her briefly before turning back to the twins, who were dropping more spaghetti onto their laps than into the mouths. Mama and Joe laughed and cleaned up the mess. Pandy remembered when she'd spilled some pudding on the carpet at the apartment they'd had before the trailer. Mama had screamed and cried about losing the deposit. Of course her mother had just finished a bottle of vodka and Pandy wasn't as young or cute as the twins.

She gazed at the other people around them, believing that when they looked at Mama, Joe, the twins and her, they must be thinking what a nice-looking family. If only it could be that way.

She found herself frequently upstaged by the adorable small children but that was okay. She had never seen her mother look so radiant, especially her blue eyes. Her skin was clear and her hair was shiny and beautiful. Pandy felt a wave of pride. She was an entirely different woman than the one who had lived in the ratty trailer with Pandy and the uncles.

It was a pleasant meal. Mama said little but Pandy caught her mother staring at her twice, and when their eyes met Mama quickly looked away. She couldn't understand it.

After an hour the twins were whining and no amount of funny gestures or silly faces would appease them. Joe started to collect their things and she looked at her mother.

"Can I see you guys again while you're in town?"

Mama sighed. "I don't think so, baby. We've got to drive out to Casa Grande tomorrow to visit Joe's folks and then after Christmas we're taking the girls to Disneyland. I'd love to invite you but we're going straight back to Salt Lake after that."

She nodded, a huge lump forming in her throat. "That's okay. It's not a big deal."

Suddenly her mother gripped her shoulder. "I'm so glad you understand, Pandora. You're so strong."

She walked them to their car and kissed the twins goodbye. She held out her hand to Joe but he surprised her and pulled her into a bear hug before climbing into the driver's seat. She stood there awkwardly in the parking lot with her mother, the December air pricking at her skin.

"Well, I guess this is goodbye again," Mama said. "You've got your cell phone, right? You can call your grandfather for a ride?"

She nodded.

Her mother looked away but Pandy could see the tears in her eyes. "I can't believe how grown up you are. You don't even need me."

Before she could respond her mother ducked into the car and shut the door. Pandy watched Joe pull away, the taillights glowing a Christmas red.

Chapter Nine

Faye brought the last of the groceries into the kitchen and stepped on Unlucky's tail. He cried and bolted out the door.

"Sorry, kitty," she called.

Andi closed the refrigerator and said, "I've never seen an animal with such an appropriate name." She took one of the bags from Faye's arms and placed it on the counter with the rest of the sacks. "How many people are coming to this shindig?"

"Eleven, counting our friends."

"And why are we having a New Year's Eve party instead of spending it alone in bed?"

Faye kissed her. "Because as scary as the thought may be, I want you to meet my family. I think you'll love my niece and nephew."

Andi grinned and Faye melted inside. She could fall in

love with her. They'd avoided the deep discussions, choosing to focus on fun, sex and work. Nearly six months had passed and neither of them had suggested renting a U-Haul. They saw each other as a complement to their very full individual lives, not a necessity.

"You'd better give me the back story on these folks before they get here. I don't want to offend anybody or jeopardize your part of the inheritance."

She chuckled. "There's nothing left to inherit. Our parents are dead and now it's just me, Rob and Elise."

"And you're not out to Elise, right?"

"Yeah. Elise and great-aunt Nell are the only two people who have no idea that I'm gay. And great-aunt Nell lives in a rest home in Florida and drools."

Andi shook her head. "How can that be, babe? You're close to Elise, right?"

Her expression soured. "Define *close*. If you mean do we live in the same town, yes. Do we attend the same family functions and normally avoid shouting matches? Yes, that's true, too. We're far too civilized to shout. But if you're asking if I share the same core values with my big sister, who still believes George Bush was right about Iraq, has Rush Limbaugh's show programmed into her satellite car radio and thinks that most poor people really could pull themselves up by their proverbial bootstraps, à la Andrew Carnegie? No, I have nothing in common with Elise."

"You make her sound awful," Andi said, putting away the last of the groceries.

"She's not awful. She's a model conservative Republican. You'll love her if you don't mention politics and she'll spend the entire time gushing over your cute shoes and quizzing you about where you like to shop. It's even occurred to me that my sister will probably like you more than me."

Andi laughed heartily but when Faye shrugged, she asked, "Are you serious?"

"Yes."

"And what about gays? What will she say if I ask her about 'Don't Ask, Don't Tell,' or if I mention Ellen DeGeneres?"

She wasn't sure. The few times when gay rights came up in the course of family discussions, she or Rob had shifted the conversation to another topic, unwilling to dwell on a landmine. She guessed that Mitch, Elise's husband, had to suspect. He was a brain surgeon, after all. And he was quiet, an observer. Whereas Elise was always far too caught up in gossip or her career to notice the changing women who entered Faye's life, Mitch always smiled knowingly. She wondered if he'd shared his suspicions with his wife but Elise always seemed clueless when she met one of Faye's lovers.

"So, how are you going to introduce me?"

It was obvious to Faye that Andi had no understanding of lesbian subterfuge in the personal arena. All of her experience with closets was professional. "I'll introduce you as a friend, of course. Why do you think I invited Jonnie, Pete, Mary Lou and Brenda?"

The light went on in Andi's head. "You're kidding. They're camouflage?"

She held up her hands. "Everyone needs a purpose."

When Andi stomped away in indignation, Faye smoothed the waters by offering her a foot rub, which led to their last sex of the calendar year.

Faye had arranged for Jonnie to arrive before her sister and as she answered the doorbell, she found Jonnie on the front porch with her brother.

"Look who I just met," Jonnie said, offering a friendly smack against Rob's shoulder. "Faye, I think you should properly introduce us."

Rob stared at Jonnie with a silly expression on his face and Faye almost laughed.

"Rob, this is Jonnie Clark, my counselor and Jonnie, this is my brother, Rob."

Jonnie extended her free hand and they both chuckled, clearly embarrassed. Faye noticed they each held a bag with a six-pack and a bottle of wine respectively. She also saw the expression on her brother's face when her hot young counselor brushed against him. She smiled slightly at the idea that her brother might have a thing for Jonnie.

"C'mon in. You guys are here first."

"Of course we are," Rob murmured. "You need buffers to hide Andi before Elise gets here."

Jonnie turned to Faye with a playful grin. "Is that what we are? Lesbian buffers?"

"Oh, yes," Rob answered. "That's really what straight people are for. They help their gay siblings stay in the closet."

They all laughed and she gazed adoringly at Rob. They were physically similar, both with dark curly hair and a slim physique, although he was slimmer. He was forty-three and their close proximity in age united them against their parents, who had used their births as last-ditch attempts to save their failing marriage.

Pete and his wife Mary Lou arrived shortly after, along with Faye's friend, Brenda. When the doorbell sounded one last time, Faye could hear her niece and nephew arguing on the porch.

"Hello!" Elise exclaimed. Her arms were filled with New Year's Eve party favors. "I've brought one for everyone including your new friend. Now, is it Andi with an 'I' or is it a 'Y'? I glittered each person's name on a horn, so I hope 'I' was correct."

Before Faye could respond Lindsay pecked her on the cheek and Alec came from behind and wrapped his arms around her.

"How's my favorite aunt?"

He grinned and Faye saw how much he looked like Elise. He had her model-like face and light auburn hair.

"I'm fine," she said, kissing him on the cheek.

"I like your new *friend*."

"Shush," she warned.

Jonnie and Rob joined them and Alec added, "Uncle Rob says you're gonna tell mom on her birthday."

"I'm not promising anything. I'm not sure she can take it."

Rob scoffed. "Of course she can take it. Our older sister is in better shape than we are. She does Pilates like a madwoman."

"That's not what I mean. And I'm not sure it's appropriate. It's her birthday. I shouldn't upstage her like that or send her into heart failure."

Alec cleared his throat and garbled, "Bullshit."

She elbowed him in the ribs before they mingled. She found Mitch in a corner watching football and said hello. After a few sentences of casual conversation she excused herself, having fulfilled her duties as sister-in-law.

Elise immediately found Andi and Faye watched them closely. She poured two glasses of chardonnay and injected herself into their conversation by handing each a wineglass.

"How do you know Faye?" Elise asked.

"She and I work together in the district. I'm the special education director."

"Oh, that sounds like a very difficult job," Elise said seriously. "I've read a lot about special education and there seems to be so many laws to understand."

Andi nodded. "The laws are ever-changing and there's always the question of funding since it costs so much."

Faye took shallow breaths and felt her heartbeat return to normal. *Crisis averted.* She drifted away when Andi steered the conversation back to Elise's charity work. Once her sister focused on herself Faye knew the chance of discussing politics or social issues was zero. There was even less of a chance they would ever mention her name again.

She wandered over to Pete and Mary Lou, who were making margaritas in the kitchen.

"Want one?" Mary Lou asked, holding up a glass.

She nodded, wide-eyed. "You bet."

Pete twisted a glass rim onto the plate of salt and filled it to the top. She took a hefty drink and felt the tequila immediately. He made a great margarita. A peal of laughter filled the room and she turned to see Elise and Andi laughing hysterically. Elise made another comment and they laughed harder.

"Your sister seems to be getting along with Andi," Pete observed.

She looked at Pete, who wore an amused expression, having guessed at their relationship a month before. "No comments, please. Just keep the margaritas coming."

Dinner proved quite pleasant especially when Brenda took over, warming the guests with her endless anecdotes about all of the famous people she encountered at the Scottsdale spa where she worked as a masseuse.

"So, is Angelina Jolie *really* that beautiful?" Lindsay asked.

"Of course," Brenda confirmed. "Her face is incredible and those lips are to die for."

"I think it's her skin," Elise commented. She looked at Andi. "Andi, you're the same way. You have flawless skin. What's your secret?"

Faye thought she might spew the end of her third margarita all over the table. She also noticed her brother and Jonnie, who had conveniently chosen seats next to each other, were now whispering and giggling.

"Well, Elise," Andi replied, "I think it's my good genes. Texans tend to eat plenty of red meat and fried foods so I can't claim to know anything about healthy living. I just enjoy life. Maybe it's because I try to keep my stress level down." Andi shot Faye a glance and she dropped her gaze to her plate.

Elise nodded. "I like your attitude, Andi. Faye, I'm glad you invited this woman. She's just like your other friends—pure class."

"Hear, hear," Pete said, raising his margarita in salute. "To great friends."

The others followed and Andi grasped her hand underneath the table and squeezed. The touch was reassuring and Faye met her gaze and smiled. If Elise noticed, Faye decided she didn't care.

When midnight had come and gone, the booze consumed, and the guests departed, Faye dropped onto the sofa and closed her eyes. Jonnie and Rob had left together. He'd be getting a phone call from her first thing in the morning. The biggest surprise had been Andi and Elise's bonding, which continued throughout the evening and culminated in an enormous hug and a promise of lunch as the Benedict clan exited.

Andi snuggled against her. "I had a great time. Your sister and brother are great. Mitch is a nice guy and your niece and nephew are incredibly sweet."

She chuckled. "Yes, they are." She didn't bother to open her eyes but she breathed deeply, enjoying Andi's perfume.

"Faye, why haven't you told Elise?"

Faye gazed at her shrewdly. "I'll answer that if you'll tell me why you left Portland."

Andi scowled and stared at the ceiling. There was no way to avoid the conversation. She said nothing and Faye thought she was employing a new strategy—silence. Faye tangled her fingers in Andi's silky hair amazed at its softness and enthralled by her nearness. She loved these moments almost as much as sex, when they'd lie in bed or on the couch existing as one, still and peaceful.

She'd given up on the question when Andi propped herself up on an elbow. "You're not gonna let this go, are you?"

"Why should I be the only one on the hot seat? Quid pro quo. If Portland was so great, why'd you leave?"

"A relationship gone bad," she said. "I got dumped."

"And that made you leave the whole city?" Faye asked skeptically. Andi had admitted to several lovers so she wasn't buying it.

Andi chewed on her lip. There was obviously more. "My dad got sick, *is* still sick with cancer. I can't be that far away anymore in case Momma needs me. It's a nonstop plane flight from here to Dallas and a short car ride. Coming from Portland almost took a day."

She thought she already knew the answer but she asked, "Why didn't you move back to Texas?"

Andi glanced at her and her serious expression cracked slightly. "That'd be *too* close. I escaped once and like a fool, I vowed I'd never come back when that Greyhound pulled out of the terminal. Stupid," she muttered. "You always go home. You have to."

"What'd you escape from?"

She shook her head. "There are so many ways to answer that question but the simplest answer and the one I'm not too tired to give is that I escaped before they found out I wasn't their perfect little girl."

Faye couldn't believe it. "Your parents don't know you're gay?"

"Nope."

Faye didn't say the obvious. She didn't call Andi a hypocrite or grow indignant from Andi's obvious double standard. Instead she kissed her forehead and pulled her closer.

"I don't know why I haven't told Elise. I can't explain it. It's not like I'm looking for her approval."

"Are you sure?" Andi asked.

She paused. "No. You know it wasn't always like this between us. When we were really little Elise was the babysitter. She got stuck with us when our parents went out and we idolized her. She was the older sister with the cool ideas. She was the one who let us camp out in the backyard and told us ghost stories. Before she went to college we spent the weekends together while our parents tried to save their marriage. It didn't work."

"When did they get divorced?"

"When I was eleven. By then Elise was almost twenty. She'd gone to Northwestern at nineteen and she didn't come back except for Christmases. She didn't see what Rob and I saw. She didn't understand what was happening to the family. When she visited we fought."

"What happened?"

"We all got older. When she went away, she changed. She lived for the sorority that my father paid for and they were a bunch of snobs. Wore pearls to bed. Then she met Mitch and started hanging out with this elite crowd full of doctors' wives, joining Junior League and talking about charity balls. They got married and she went on with her career, the high life, the whole thing."

"Where were you and Rob?"

"We were right here. We never left. They lived in Chicago and we hardly saw her. Everything is a choice and Elise always chose something else—the vacation in Paris, the charity event that she couldn't miss and the big business deal she had to close. It was all more important than us."

"But she moved back here."

"Because she got a great job offer."

"Do you think that's the only reason?"

"Yeah."

Andi was quiet for a long time and Faye began to wonder if she'd fallen asleep until she said, "You could be wrong, honey. She may have finally realized how important it was to be close to you."

She sat up and stared at her. "Whose side are you on?"

Andi caressed her cheek and smiled. "I'm on your side, baby. Only yours. You want me to hog-tie her and roast her on a spit, I'll do it. I'll go round me up some gringos and we'll make the little lady pay."

Chapter Ten

The heavy traffic from Camelback Road signaled the comings and goings of the New Year's Eve revelers. Horns honked endlessly and twice Constance heard tires squeal—but no crash—as cars avoided each other. She'd opened the patio door to let some air in, convinced that the condo seemed stuffy. At least that's what she told herself. The noise below created a connection with other people, something she'd lacked for the past week.

She hated the days between Christmas and New Year's. Everyone wanted the time off. Many of her employees saved their personal time just so they could spend that precious week with their families, which meant there was no point in trying to work. She'd given up fighting it. Three years before her office manager had succinctly told her that if she wanted to keep her employees happy, she'd close the office. So she did.

"Good for them," she said, draining her wineglass.

She glanced at the empty wine bottle and debated whether to find another or continue relaxing in the dark. Armour was fast asleep, having exhausted himself playing with his toys all day.

That was the one positive to Christmas. It gave her a reason to shower him with gifts that amused him endlessly for days. At least she could rest in peace. And she'd busied herself with many activities that week. She'd read a book, reorganized her closet and drafted a pleading for her first case after the holidays. She'd even hired a sitter for an afternoon and shopped. It had been a productive week.

Ira never called. She frowned at the thought of losing his companionship but it was probably for the best. She went to the kitchen to open another bottle of pinot noir and glanced at the picture of Cora that perched on the counter.

There were pictures of Cora throughout the condo. She wanted her all around. This one always made her smile because it showed Cora climbing the ladder to their tree house, their secret place. They'd spend hours in the tree house their father had built for them at their mother's urging. June believed all children needed a place to be themselves, away from adults. And when she was alive Buck would do anything to please his wife. He'd erected the fortress in the giant oak tree that divided their property from the Mumford's land. The place was Cora's stage and Constance was an audience of one while she belted out the hits of the day from memory.

"Sing "Gypsies, Tramps and Thieves," again!" Constance begged her sister, who was as talented as she was beautiful. She'd laughed and sung the song from memory while Constance swayed to the music.

She adored Cora, who was five years older and everything she longed to be. Cora had won the school talent show three times. Tall, with beautiful flaxen hair, she possessed shiny eyes and creamy skin. She was the image of their beautiful mother, who'd chosen their father over a string of beaus.

She could've been a cover girl for any one of the movie

magazines they stashed in the tree house. They'd lay on their stomachs side by side and flip through the pages, commenting on how much they loved the movie *Love Story* or how handsome Sean Connery was in *Diamonds are Forever.* They both agreed that Audrey Hepburn was *the* most beautiful woman on earth.

"I think you're just as pretty as her," she'd once told Cora.

Cora had blushed and laughed. "You're my biggest fan, Con." She kissed her on the head. "When I move to Hollywood, I'll take you with me. I'll never leave you here."

She tottered back into the living room, well aware that she was drunk but not caring in the slightest. A knock at the front door made her jump. She made no effort to answer it, as the doorman would have called her if a guest had arrived. When the knocking turned to pounding, she rushed to the peephole, worried that the noise would wake Armour.

Ira stood outside, his hands in his pockets. He looked horrible and she suspected he was drunk as well. Her fiery wrath peaked and she pulled open the door.

"What the hell are you doing here? Why did Joseph let you up?"

"Joseph actually *likes* me, a concept I know is foreign to you. Now, I've come here tonight to celebrate with you. How about a friendly fuck for a happy new year?"

"You're drunk," she said, throwing the door shut, but he stepped in its path and pushed inside.

He had enough sense to close the door quietly before he faced her. His expression was unreadable but she realized that she didn't know him. She'd never made any attempt to learn his habits, his peccadilloes, even his temper.

"I think you should go home," she said softly, almost afraid.

"I don't think so."

"Ira—"

He covered the distance between them in an instant and grabbed her wrists. He was incredibly strong and to fight him would only bring injury. She let him pull her against his chest and she smelled the strong odor of bourbon.

"Have you been enjoying the gift I sent you?"

"All evening."

"Did you go skiing?"

"Yup."

She couldn't contain her jealousy. "Is she pretty?"

He laughed. "Actually, she *is* pretty. She's my niece. I took her and my sister to the slopes for *their* Christmas present. Then I came home and got drunk. How's that for a merry fucking Christmas?"

She gazed into his hooded eyes illuminated by the moonlight and saw the sadness she'd created. He no longer seemed dangerous and she relaxed. He'd gotten drunk over her. He hadn't spent the holidays with another woman—only his family—and that was because she'd refused to spend time with him. Normally she felt a sense of triumph when she trampled over people's emotions, an incredible vindication and superiority. Yet standing in the dark with him she felt neither.

"Please let go of my wrists."

He complied, his arms falling at his side, his head hung. She burrowed her fingers through his hair and closed her eyes, as his arms slid around her, enraptured by his touch, his nearness. In a single embrace the accomplishments of the week were diminished, incomparable. Every ridiculous task had done nothing but fill her time. She'd missed him terribly and felt incredible regret that they'd been apart.

She kissed his cheek and whispered, "Make love to me."

Chapter Eleven

The early morning January chill felt wonderful to Pandy. Having spent awful winters in Utah, she would never think of Arizona as cold. It was brisk in a friendly way that made the blood pump, but in Utah winter was dark and often deadly. She lay on the sidewalk next to the Cedar Hills front gate, staring at a few billowy clouds that dotted the light blue sky, the cold creeping up her spine. The concrete grew uncomfortable, almost painful, but she didn't move. It was her favorite kind of pain—a type that didn't leave suspicious marks.

She knew she had to be careful now. After the dinner with her mother she'd gone home and cut herself several times, once too deeply. Grandpa had rushed her to the hospital and they'd put her on suicide watch for a few days. The resident psychiatrist had asked her if she wanted to die. When she said no, the tired woman nodded and prescribed some antidepressants that Pandy refused to take. Now she was stuck going to talk therapy once a week, which seemed utterly pointless since the shrink let her pick the topics. So far they'd had several deep conversations about *Catcher in the Rye* and that was okay with her. At least the woman wasn't poking around in her childhood.

She flipped open her cell and called Brian but it went right to voice mail. She wasn't surprised since he'd left her house around midnight after they'd watched *The Rocky Horror Picture Show* for the eighteenth time and spent an hour more debating which celebrities they'd gladly lose their virginity to.

Voices broke the silence and she quickly sat up. Two boys climbed over a nearby fence, laughing and talking in Spanish. She guessed they'd been messing around on the school grounds. Cedar Hills was only protected by simple chain link and people constantly scaled the fences to shoot hoops or have beer parties on the weekend. She'd seen all kinds of trash on the field, including used condoms, beer cans and fast-food wrappers.

They saw her and immediately stopped talking. She recognized them as Poncho and Turtle, obviously not their real names but their gang names. They wore the typical Dickies pants, work shirts, L.A. Clippers caps and blue bandannas wrapped around their knees like tourniquets. Poncho whispered to Turtle and she imagined they were trying to decide whether to hassle her. She knew it could get pretty rough. She reached into her bag for her Swiss army knife and set it in her lap, resting her sketchpad over it.

"Hey, girl," Poncho said. "Whatcha doin' out here?"

She buried her hands under the sketchpad and opened the blade. They were close enough now that she could see their smiles of trouble and she knew that they particularly enjoyed messing up the gay kids. One of her friends had been fondled in the bathroom by a Hispanic girl who was rumored to be the bitch of the Sixteenth Street gang leader. Fear of those confrontations was the main reason she never used the school restrooms except in the office when she visited Ms. Clark.

A van rumbled into the school parking lot and the two boys quickly changed direction and disappeared over an adjacent wall. She sighed and closed her knife at the sight of

Ms. Taylor's ancient VW Microbus. She saw Ms. Clark sitting in the passenger's seat, and when she saw Pandy, she waved. None of the other students had arrived yet and Pandy suddenly felt like a huge loser, the only student who'd bothered to show up on time for the mural painting. Now she was stuck with the adults by herself. But she loved Ms. Clark and Ms. Taylor was entirely cool, dressed in ripped jeans and a T-shirt that read DIVA across the chest. She didn't understand the message but maybe Ms. Taylor loved opera.

She went to help them unload the supplies and Ms. Clark embraced her. "I'm so glad this is happening, Pandy. You're so talented. I just know the mural will be beautiful."

She nodded, slightly embarrassed. If anyone else had praised her that much, she would have known they were lying just to keep her happy. Because everyone wanted her happy now. After the cutting incident all of her teachers suddenly gave her breaks with missed assignments and they looked at her like a dog left at the shelter. Only Ms. Clark and Ms. Taylor were genuine. Everyone else was a phony.

"Hey, Pandy," Ms. Taylor called with a slight wave. "Can you help me with these paints?" she asked.

She unloaded the pallet onto a dolly and they wheeled the supplies into the amphitheater area where the white wall awaited their creativity. She really was excited about the mural but she didn't want anyone to know. The central image was a rainbow but within the rainbow would be many faces to represent various ethnicities and even a few religious symbols like Jesus, Buddha and a menorah. At the end of the rainbow would be the world instead of a pot of gold.

Ms. Taylor instructed her to start outlining the mural in pencil, paying careful attention to scale since everything needed to be much larger than her original drawing. Eventually other students from the art class joined them but she worked alone. They all chatted and gossiped but she remained quiet. They weren't her friends and she didn't hang with any of them during lunch. None of the kids she knew would ever be caught dead at school on a Saturday morning. They were all home asleep right now.

The sun quickly destroyed the enjoyable morning chill and the concrete amphitheater was an oven, thoroughly baking them. By lunchtime beads of sweat were dripping from her forehead.

Someone tapped her on the arm. She turned to find a bottle of water under her nose. "Hey, do you want a drink?"

She stood up and faced Sonia, the student council president. "Sure. Thanks."

She opened the bottle, avoiding Sonia's gaze. They'd had a few classes together but she always thought Sonia had no idea she existed. She was the perfect blond beauty with gorgeous blue eyes and long tanned legs. In addition to being student council president, she had played for the volleyball and basketball teams. She seemed to have the perfect life and Pandy felt totally unworthy to stand in her presence.

"It's looking great," Sonia said. "I love your design."

"Thanks."

Her heart pounded and she had no idea why. All they were doing was talking. She'd heard good things about Sonia and how she was genuinely kind to kids who weren't part of her group. Pandy decided she wasn't a phony. When she glanced at Sonia again, Sonia smiled and her eyes seemed to sparkle. Suddenly she felt light-headed and she didn't think she could speak.

"Well, I better get back over there. You know how Taylor is about lazy asses." Sonia returned to the cluster of students on the opposite side of the mural.

"Hey, Pandy, come on up here and bring your sketchpad," Ms. Taylor called.

She joined Ms. Taylor at the top of the amphitheater's hill that overlooked the mural.

"I think we may have a problem. We're still going to have some unused space toward the bottom right corner. What would you like to do with that area?"

She shrugged. "I don't know."

"Then you better sit down young lady and come up with an idea. This is your project." She walked away leaving Pandy alone with her thoughts.

She dropped to the grass and stared at the wall, the white cement partially covered in swirls and patches of color. She couldn't help but smile. It was going to be amazing but Ms. Taylor was right. They had a bald area that needed to be filled for balance.

She flipped her pad open to a new page and watched Sonia bend over to dip her brush in a paint jar. As if she could sense Pandy was spying, Sonia turned and met her stare. She smiled and Pandy snapped her eyes down to the paper on her lap. How could she be so stupid? Sonia would think she was some sort of perv. She started to cry and Sonia's smile cast a veil over her mind. Her hands were moving but she couldn't see what images filled the page. It was as if she were blind and all she saw was Sonia smiling—no, laughing—at her stupidity.

Undoubtedly by Monday morning the entire eighth grade would be snickering when she walked down the hall, all of them knowing that the gay girl had checked out the school president. Her stomach churned and she thought she might throw up but she didn't move, except for her right hand, which continued to draw, littering the page with pencil marks.

Someone touched her shoulder and she nearly jumped a foot in the air.

"I'm so sorry," Ms. Clark said. "I didn't mean to scare you. Are you okay?"

Ms. Clark sat down next to her and she nodded, wiping away the tears that covered her cheeks. "It's okay. I just didn't know you were there."

"I was watching you, and sweetie, I think we're going to need to have a talk."

She looked at Ms. Clark, puzzled. "About what?"

Ms. Clark pointed to the sketchpad. "About your drawings."

She'd drawn a landscape of a beautiful hilly field with trees and birds. It looked serene except for the stark image that sat in the center of the picture—a young girl lying in a coffin, her eyes closed and her arms crossed over her chest. The girl looked like Pandy and a name was written across the bottom.

Ms. Clark stared at the picture for a long time before asking, "Pandy, who's Athena?"

Chapter Twelve

Faye decided that it would be a very long day. The Friday before spring break was always chaotic since the third quarter was about to end and both students and staff needed some time off. In the three hours she'd been on the job, she'd broken up a fight on the basketball court, settled a dispute between two staff members and been tortured by a thirty-minute phone conversation with Dr. Marjorie.

"Oh, Faye," she'd gushed. "You should be so proud of your students. They did such marvelous work on the mural."

She quietly tapped on her keyboard, answering e-mail while they talked. "Thanks, Marjorie. Pandy Webber was the student who thought of the idea. She's a different kid so I'm glad we could honor her."

"It's terrific but I need to give you a little heads-up."

She stopped typing. A little heads-up was Marjorie's way of negating every positive word she'd just uttered and whatever problem she was alluding to would undoubtedly consume hours of Faye's life and lead to an entire reversal of fortune.

"Go ahead."

"Well, I've had a few phone calls from some parents who've seen it and they're a little concerned about the religious overtones and the inclusion of the rainbow."

She took a deep breath and played stupid. "I understand why the religious symbols might raise eyebrows but what's wrong with the rainbow?"

"Now, Faye, don't jump too far overboard here. They understand that there are many ways to interpret rainbows but you and I both know that the rainbow is an emblem for gay pride, among other things."

"Really?, I wasn't aware of that," she replied drolly.

Marjorie chuckled at her humor. "Right. I reassured the parents that the rainbow was part of a visual symbol representing all ethnicities, you know, all the colors of the rainbow."

"In other words, you made sure they believed that it wasn't associated with gay diversity."

Marjorie paused at her bluntness. She hated confrontation. "Faye, I don't know what that young lady meant when she created it and I don't think I need to know—"

"She's a gay student, Marjorie."

"So?"

"So the rainbow *does* represent everything the parents fear. I just want you to be clear about that. The point of the mural is to celebrate all types of diversity—sexual, racial and religious. Pandy Webber did a great job of including everyone."

Marjorie sighed deeply. "Faye, saying these things to me over the phone is fine. You're frustrated, you don't think the parents should have a problem with this and I don't either. But you and I both know that this isn't a molehill that we want to see grow into Mount Everest. We need to make this go away. Like everything else eventually all the hoopla will die down. For now, though, I need you to toe the company line and keep our rear ends out of the fire."

She stared at the stress ball in her hand, counting the number of euphemisms Marjorie had already used. "And what's the company line? Just so I'm clear."

"It's all about ethnic diversity. Leave everything else out, okay?"

"If I'm asked directly I won't lie. Are you okay if I just deflect all comments about this? Start talking about something else and create a diversion?"

"Of course you can. You're a master at diversion. I mean look at your relationship with Andi."

She nearly dropped the phone on the desk. "What are you talking about?"

"Oh, c'mon, Faye," she said, her voice barely above a whisper. "The entire district office knows about you two. No other principal calls Andi as much as you do. Didn't you think Estella would pick up on it?"

Estella was Andi's faithful secretary, and while Faye and Andi had been meticulously careful since the night of the board meeting, she wondered what Estella knew and what Dr. Marjorie had seen.

"Look," Marjorie continued, "it's not like anyone cares. We all love you and Andi and we want you to be happy. Just don't be obvious."

The weight of her words hit Faye. Marjorie Machabell had drawn a nice little pink triangle with Faye, Andi and the mural as the three points. She wanted to make sure that the points remained unconnected or there could be problems. Amid the circuitousness of her argument, Faye finally found the destination—Bill Gleeson.

"I take it that our new superintendent *doesn't* know about Andi's and my relationship?"

"No, he's clueless for now. Even I was surprised to find out about Andi, but frankly Faye, you don't fit his leadership paradigm."

"Excuse me?"

Dead silence filled time and she imagined Marjorie was choosing her words carefully. "It's just that Bill has a set idea of how a principal looks and acts. Not that women can't be principals," she quickly added. "He's on board with the idea of women in power."

"Thank God," Faye said. "I'd hate to tell him we can vote, too."

"Now, Faye," Marjorie reprimanded. "I just want you to be careful. You look like a lesbian and you run a tough school. Don't add this mural issue to the fire. It's already hot enough with this Constance Richardson thing. Am I clear? You don't want to lose your seat on the bus."

Faye was momentarily speechless. Marjorie had abandoned her usual marshmallow outlook on the world where everything was twinkling lights and lovely pastel colors. Rarely did she speak this harshly and Faye recognized she was trying to do her a favor.

"I understand. I'll always do my best to support the district."

"I know you will. Now, about this complaint from the state. I'm sure Andi's told you that the auditor they sent has taken up much of her time, requesting documents and reviewing protocols. Frankly, Faye, it's as if the entire Glen Oaks special education department is under fire, particularly Andi. This isn't about one little boy. You do realize that, don't you?"

"I understand the issues, Marjorie."

And she did. The investigation had consumed their lives. Andi's stress level had tripled as she tried to do her job and please the auditor at the same time. All of the other children in Glen Oaks took a back seat to Constance Richardson.

"I mention all of this because I need to prepare you. We're going to revisit this entire situation after spring break. Bill may want to go in a different direction."

Warning lights flashed in her mind and she pictured A.J. smashing a student with a bat.

"Go on," she said simply. "Does that mean he'll be in Coach Fleming's P.E. class?"

"We'll see," Marjorie hedged. "Nothing's definite. Are you going anywhere for spring break?" she asked, signaling the professional part of the phone call was concluded.

"Um, I'm going on a cruise to the Caribbean."

"My gosh, you'll just love it. Have you or Andi been on a cruise?"

She paused, taken aback by Marjorie's correct assumptions. While it wasn't unusual for her to ask personal questions, Faye had never had a conversation with Marjorie that included her lover by name.

"Uh, no. It's a first for both of us."

"Well, you have a great time and we'll see you in a week."

She debated whether she should tell Andi that most of the district was aware of their relationship. Inevitably it would ruin their vacation if Andi learned their secret was out. She was positive that Estella wasn't directly responsible for the leak since she was incredibly loyal to Andi. Most likely Marjorie had seen their affection on the night of the board meeting and decided to squeeze Estella for information. Marjorie Machabell was a gossip whore who freely manipulated her power.

As they climbed into her truck for the drive to the airport, Faye wrestled with her guilt until Andi made a pronouncement.

"Let's make a pact. Nothing about work."

"Nothing?"

"Yup. I don't want to hear about kids, parents, problems or Constance Richardson. Whoever brings up any Glen Oaks topics has to eat a whole plate of Rocky Mountain oysters."

Faye made a face at the thought of chewing on bull testicles. "Have you ever had that dish?"

Andi nodded with a wry grin. "I have indeed but fortunately I was too drunk to remember it."

Forgetting about Glen Oaks proved incredibly easy. They'd taken an Olivia Cruise to be away from every hetero they knew and amid snorkeling in the warm ocean water, sunning on the beach, dancing in the nightclubs and incredibly hot sex in their cabin, she thought of nothing significant.

On the fourth day of the cruise, she had a fleeting thought about her calendar for the next week while they soaked in the

Jacuzzi until Andi's hand, hidden by the whirling foam, caressed the inside of her thigh and headed for parts unknown. Cedar Hills vanished immediately.

"What are you thinking about, honey?" Andi asked one night as they strolled around the Promenade deck in the moonlight. "And it better not be about *that place.*"

She really wasn't thinking, only feeling. For the first time in years, her senses took over, and she breathed in the sea, tasted the salt in her mouth and felt Andi's warm hand in her own. How could she explain that?

"I'm just enjoying this trip so much. It's probably the best vacation I've ever had."

Andi beamed. The Caribbean cruise had been her idea. "I knew you'd love it. It's so beautiful here."

"It's not just that. I love being with you like this. I don't want to go home in two days."

"After this, who would?"

She shook her head. An epiphany was dawning and she needed to share it. She held Andi tightly in her arms, hoping she conveyed the right sense of urgency. "It's more than that. Having all this fun has reminded me of so many things. It's weird. It's not as if I've never laughed or had a good time but it's like I've been wearing the wrong prescription in my glasses and suddenly I can see again." She gazed at Andi's knowing expression. "Okay, so maybe that's a terrible simile. It's not like I was an English teacher. I taught high school math. We don't know how to explain things very well."

Andi gently kissed her forehead. "You're explaining it just fine, darlin'," she said in her wonderful drawl. "As granny would say, you're wound as tight as a too-small bathing suit on a long ride home from the beach. Tell me what you see."

"I hate my job."

"I know. And you're gonna need to do something about that, honey." She ran her fingers through Faye's hair and kissed her again. "But we're not having that conversation now or you'll be enjoying a nice steaming plate of oysters." They moved together for a kiss and Andi murmured, "Baby, I love you."

Faye closed her eyes and she knew she was smiling through

the kiss. In this moment devoid of analysis, thought, concern and anxiety, the words made total sense. There was nothing surrounding her heart, no walls and no shields. Andi had picked the most perfect moment possible to share her feelings. *Talk about timing.*

"I love you, too, honey."

She thought she could hear music through the kiss that followed and only an abrupt jostling from the sea startled them and separated their lips. They held each other to avoid falling into a heap on the deck, laughing at their own clumsiness.

When they'd righted themselves, Andi said, "I guess this means we're officially a couple."

Faye grinned. "I guess so."

"When can I move in?"

Faye's grin dissolved instantly and Andi chuckled.

"I'm only kidding, honey. I know you'd rather eat those Rocky Mountain oysters than rent a U-Haul."

Chapter Thirteen

Wall-to-wall Armani and Brooks Brothers suits filled the Civic Plaza ballroom for the annual Legal Aid luncheon and awards ceremony. Constance stood in the doorway and surveyed the scene. Only lawyers would wear such dark, conservative clothing to a gala event, but amid the wool suits and herringbone skirts, splashes of color telegraphed a subtle message: attorneys' wardrobes generally disguised the bestial nature of their profession but the red neckties and the deep mauve blouses conveyed the kill and the carnage that they all so enjoyed.

She shivered in excitement at the sight of her colleagues who would applaud politely and enviously when she accepted one of the awards for pro bono work in the community. Of course she never met with the homeless or the indigent. She certainly didn't have time, but it was with her approval that several junior attorneys went out into the shelters each week, foregoing hundreds of billable hours for *Constance Richardson, Attorney at Law, LLP.* As the captain of the ship she deserved this award.

She worked her way through the room, chatting with her colleagues and friendly adversaries, all of whom were on their best behavior, their fangs and claws hidden to preserve the solemnity of the occasion as the Arizona Bar Foundation attempted to portray lawyers as humans. Many congratulated her and she relished the acknowledgment.

She felt a hand on her arm and a voice whispered, "You are the most beautiful woman in this room and after this is over, I'm taking you to bed. I hope your afternoon is free."

Without turning around to stare into Ira's eyes, she asked, "And what if I'm booked?"

"Clear your calendar."

He walked away but only after his hand grazed her buttocks. She shivered and finished her wine, which was already going to her head. She needed to eat soon. She wanted to be honored, hear the roar of applause from her peers and have Ira shuttle her away to the hotel.

She glanced at the clock. The president of the bar association would step to the microphone in a few minutes and direct everyone to their tables. Her afternoon was about to begin. She checked her cell phone and frowned when she saw the blinking voice mail light. She'd silenced it before entering the ballroom but force of habit made her check the message.

Her heart sank when she saw Faye Burton's familiar extension. The woman called her with every trivial problem under the sun. Couldn't they control Armour for a few lousy hours? She moved away from the din of noisy attorneys and into the hallway to replay the message. Apparently he'd been caught lying on the floor and looking up a girl's dress. She rolled her eyes. Big fucking deal. She'd had three or four boys do that to her during school and it certainly didn't warrant a phone call. Burton's message droned on about his lack of appropriate choices and she urged Constance to call her back immediately.

She pressed END. She had no intention of ruining the

afternoon to solve Faye Burton's problems. This was her time. Right now Armour was the responsibility of Cedar Hills Elementary School.

When she returned to the ballroom people were taking their seats and beginning their lunch. She quickly joined the other award recipients on the dais, noticing that they were all younger and better-looking. She glanced toward Ira, who was seated next to a gorgeous blonde. The two of them were laughing and jealousy tore through her in an instant. He looked fantastic in a dark gray suit, much different than the day he'd appeared in her office with Nick Manos. When he finally looked up and saw the expression on her face, he immediately shifted in his seat and pretended to ignore what the blonde was saying, focusing on his water glass. Constance would berate him later and he would beg for sex.

Ninety minutes later the desserts were devoured and the speeches finished, she directed an icy stare toward Ira as she swiftly left the ballroom, her engraved plaque in hand, proof of her value in the legal community. He trailed behind calling her name until they reached the parking valet outside.

"Constance, look at me," he said, short of breath from sprinting after her. He handed the valet his ticket and stepped in front of her.

"Leave me the hell alone," she said with little forcefulness. She gazed into his eyes and her knees went weak. There was something about him—something so good, something she'd lost long ago.

A wave of attorneys joined them at the curb, waiting for the attendants to retrieve their Lexuses, Mercedes and BMWs. They all exchanged meaningless banter, critiquing the poor meal and ridiculing the bar president who chronically laced his orations with pointless stories. She absently participated in the dialogue, her attention focused on Ira's hand, which was wrapped around her waist. Surrounded by their peers he had chosen this moment to claim her as his own. She suppressed a schoolgirl giggle that desperately wanted to burst from her mouth as she watched her colleagues' eyes move quizzically from her to him, a man much younger than she. They were shocked that the Steamroller had bagged such a prize.

When his BMW convertible pulled in front of them, he guided her to the passenger's side and she didn't protest. They pulled away and his free hand rested on her thigh.

"I thought I told you to leave me alone?"

He laughed. "Sweetheart, you should know by now that I don't listen to a word that comes out of your mouth. I watch your eyes."

She smiled at him, supremely pleased. "Thank God."

She leaned against the leather headrest, enjoying his touch, imagining the afternoon that lay ahead and realizing this was one of the best days she could remember in a long time. Her cell phone chimed and she scowled. She should have turned it off.

"Please don't answer that," he said.

"I don't have a choice. I told Melanie the luncheon ended at two. She may have some questions about a depo I took this morning." She glanced at the display and saw Faye Burton's extension. "Damn it."

"What's wrong?"

"It's Armour's principal."

She put her finger on the silence button but hesitated. She could feel his gaze on her like a stick poking at her conscience. What would he think of her if she didn't answer a phone call from the school? He knew she had a disabled child but the depth of their relationship excluded details and complexities. To ignore the call would require an explanation she didn't want to give—one that could shame her.

"Constance Richardson."

"Ms. Richardson, this is Faye Burton from Cedar Hills. I hope you got my last message about the incident with A.J. today."

"Of course. I was just about to call you back."

Ira glanced at her and she averted his judgmental stare. Burton said something but a scream cut her off. She knew that sound. It was Armour. She pulled the phone away from her ear, unable to endure his piercing wails. She glanced at Ira's mortified expression. The screams dissipated and she imagined Burton was moving to a quieter location.

"Ms. Richardson, are you still there?"

"Yes," she answered through clenched teeth. "I take it there's a problem?"

Burton chuckled. "That's putting it mildly. When we removed A.J. from the classroom for looking up the girls' skirts, he became inconsolable. He's been screaming for the past hour in our front office, and no one—not me, Mr. Salinas, Mrs. Strauss or Nurse Chang could get him to stop. We even pulled his student mentor out of class to see if she could get him to calm down. Nothing is working. I need you to come get your son."

"That's absolutely impossible."

She looked at Ira, who was completely tuned into the conversation. Burton launched into a diatribe about the importance of preserving the learning environment and she shifted in her seat. The most important and sacred piece of her personal life was on display. Ira would judge her and find her an unfit parent.

When Burton paused, she said, "Surely this can wait until the end of the school day when Cathy picks him up."

"You need to come *now*, Ms. Richardson. This is not a choice."

The commanding tone of her voice immediately put Constance on the defensive. No one spoke to her in that manner. "Ms. Burton, I am not available and I do not appreciate your tone or the fact that you feel you can give me orders. Ms. Loomis, the superintendent and the governing board will be hearing about this conversation."

A long pause ensued and she was about to hang up when Burton said slowly, "Ms. Richardson, as the administrator for Cedar Hills, I am given the authority to remove any student I believe is jeopardizing the safety of himself or others. I believe A.J. is in danger. At this moment he is thrashing about our conference room and he won't let Mr. Salinas near him. If you don't come and get your son right now, I will call the police to appropriately restrain him even if that requires the use of handcuffs. Then he will be personally delivered to your office. It's your choice."

The air left her lungs and she thought she might throw up her rubber chicken lunch. She glanced at Ira. She could tell he was upset but his eyes remained on the road.

"Fine," she answered evenly.

She snapped her phone shut and dropped it into her purse. She waited for him to say something but he remained quiet, probably calculating a way he could break up with her and rid himself of the over-the-hill bitch and her autistic banshee son.

Damn that Faye Burton! No doubt she took immense pleasure in giving ultimatums, particularly to a powerful woman who earned five times her salary and lived a life she would never have. Constance knew this was all part of their master plan to rid themselves of Armour and force him from Cedar Hills. They knew how to push his buttons and set him off.

Her cheeks burned at the thought of their cruel exploitation of her son. They were unforgiving and relentless and they had ruined her perfect afternoon, not that Ira would have been interested after listening to her phone conversation. Rage coursed through her and for a fleeting second she thought of throwing herself from the car. She steadied her emotions and folded her hands in her lap. *Faye Burton would pay. She had the proof, but she would wait patiently for the perfect time to play her trump card.*

"You need to take me back to my car," she said flatly.

Ira shrugged. "Why? We're almost to the school. Let's just go get him."

His compassion and interest in her personal life rekindled the rage inside. She thrust her body close to him and screamed, "Just take me back to my Goddamn car!"

Chapter Fourteen

The city bus was crowded when Brian and Pandy boarded for their Friday night visit to the Commons. Most of the seats were filled with middle-aged people whose droopy eyes and frowns conveyed the fatigue and stress of adulthood. As they shuffled to the back where the other students traditionally sat, Pandy decided she would never wear that expression on a Friday night. She didn't understand how anyone could be miserable on the greatest day of the week. All she saw was the celebration and the joy of being free for an entire two days from school. Fridays were even better than Saturdays when she had to do chores around the house.

The Commons was an upscale shopping mall in central Phoenix and *the* place to be on Friday night. There was a movie multiplex but a lot of the kids just hung out at the Starbucks until the security guards hassled them about loitering. She and Brian were always careful to behave and they never smoked or drank there, unlike some of the other students who often bought their pot or cocaine in the upper level of the parking garage. She knew bad things happened at the Commons but it was the hottest hangout.

The bus dropped them at Camelback Road and she could see the movie marquee across the street, towering above the surrounding high-rises. She wondered if she'd see Sonia. A few weeks before they'd both been outside Starbucks and Sonia came over to her and said hi. Pandy thought she might drop into a heap at her feet but she managed to have a semi-coherent conversation. When Sonia waved goodbye she only felt like half a loser.

"Do you think Jake will be here tonight?" Brian asked as they crossed the street.

Jake was the love of Brian's life, a high school sophomore with green hair. Unfortunately he didn't seem to know that Brian existed.

"I don't know. Maybe."

They passed Starbucks and several dark businesses that closed their doors at five and headed for the escalator to the mezzanine and the movie multiplex.

"Did you want to see anything tonight?" she asked.

Brian shrugged. "I don't know. There's that new Owen Wilson movie. It looked funny."

They went to the box office and bought their tickets. "We've still got about half an hour," Brian said, checking his watch. "Why don't we just hang for a while and see who shows up."

"Cool."

They found a bench near the escalator and began to people-watch, guessing who was gay, straight or clueless. A thin guy with Elvis Costello glasses and spiked hair swished toward the box office.

"Too easy," Brian said. "Definitely our team."

She nodded her agreement. A couple with two children ascended the escalator and she thought of her mother.

The family had just stepped off when laughter and shouts

erupted. Four boys spilled onto the mezzanine and two made a show of falling to the ground.

"Get the hell off me, homo!"

She instantly recognized the group. All of them were friends of Travis, the boy who hated Brian. Since Travis was the brains of the group she imagined he couldn't be far behind. By the time they moved away from the escalator she saw Travis, his arm possessively wrapped around Sonia.

"Crap," Brian said.

"Let's get out of here."

She started to rise but Brian grabbed her arm. "No fuckin' way. We have as much right to be here as they do."

"Brian, c'mon. We don't need any shit."

He clamped his hand down on her arm and said, "Don't let them do this."

They were already headed toward the ticket booth. *Maybe they won't notice us*, she thought. She watched Sonia's backside, amazed at how good she looked in tight white jeans.

A clatter stopped the group and Sonia turned to retrieve her purse which had fallen from her shoulder. She collected everything that had spilled onto the concrete and when she looked up, she saw Pandy.

"Hey, Pandy," she called.

Shit. She waved slightly and turned to Brian who sighed heavily.

"Here we go," he murmured.

"Well, fuckin'-A," Travis said, sauntering toward them his thumbs looped into his front pockets. He wore a Polo shirt that was a size too small and the waistband of his Joe Boxers was visible over his jeans. "What the fuck do we have here? A couple of fuckin' faggots?"

Brian grinned. "That would be impossible. If we're fucking faggots then we'd need to be the same sex. I'd have thought that even a dickwad like you would know that, Travis."

"You fuckin' asshole," he growled.

He pulled Brian up by the lapels of his trench coat and pushed him against the wall. Pandy jumped on his back and pulled his hair. She managed to get her arm wrapped around his neck before strong hands grabbed her by the shoulders and ripped her away. She fell to the ground and instantly saw stars.

"Pandy, are you okay?"

Sonia was standing over her like an angel. She heard yelling and swearing and she guessed that Brian was getting a hellacious beating but all she could do was lie there and smile at Sonia. She closed her eyes and thought she felt Sonia's hand caress her cheek. When she opened them again, Sonia was gone, replaced by Brian and a large security guard.

She sat up. "What happened?"

"Travis's friend threw you to the ground. You hit your head pretty hard."

She noticed that Brian's lower lip was bleeding. "Are you okay?"

"Yeah." He pointed at the security guard. "Merrill came to my rescue just as Travis was about to pound me."

Merrill clapped him on the back. "Lucky thing, too. He'd have beaten the crap out of you, Brian."

He scowled. "I don't think so."

They helped her stand up and Merrill waved goodbye.

"How do you know him?" she asked.

"I buy him cappuccinos and he watches my back. Great guy." He touched his lip. "Son of a bitch. Exactly the same spot as last time."

She hugged herself and looked around. Travis and his friends were gone, probably into the theater. "Let's just go."

He shook his head. "No way. I'm not letting him get away with this shit anymore. I say we go to the movies. We already paid so let's do it."

He started toward the door but she grabbed his sleeve. Pandy was almost certain Travis, Sonia and their friends would be at the same movie since it was the only one that looked interesting to teens. "Brian, please. Let's go back to my house and we can watch DVDs. I'll even watch that Joan Crawford one again. C'mon, my head is killing me."

"Nope."

Brian insisted on buying two large drinks and a tub of popcorn for their dinner before they entered the theater. She was relieved to see that the annoying commercials had already started and they could find their seats in the cover of darkness. She scanned the auditorium and pointed at two seats at the end of a row. She glanced up and saw Travis's friends sitting directly behind them in the wide row that separated the bottom and upper tier but Travis and Sonia weren't there. She heard laughter and realized that they had claimed the back corner of the top row for themselves. She swallowed hard, imagining what they were doing or would soon be doing when the movie started. All of the theaters at the Commons had blow job seats in the shadowy corners that were unofficially reserved for young couples. The thought of them together made her sick and she felt so confused. She thought Sonia was an incredible person, certainly deserving of someone better than Travis.

The previews began and she tried to focus on the screen until she noticed Sean, one of Travis's friends, trudging up the stairs to join the other thugs in their row. She almost said something to Brian but he was engrossed in the preview for a stupid teen comedy. She hoped Sean wouldn't see them in the dark but as he passed Brian, he shoved his shoulder, spilling part of Brian's drink into his lap.

"Son of a bitch," he said, reaching for the pile of napkins between them.

"Why don't we just leave?"

"Because I want to see the damn movie," he said. "We've paid our money and we're going to enjoy this."

Several nearby moviegoers shushed them as the feature began. The opening credits had barely finished when she felt something hit her neck. She brushed it away but she guessed the boys were throwing Raisinets or Milk Duds. She glanced at Brian who shifted in his seat uncomfortably. Obviously he was being assaulted as well. It was pointless to try to watch the film. Every time she started to follow the dialogue, a spit-covered candy hit her in the head.

"I'm going to the bathroom," she whispered and headed down the stairs. She was furious with Brian, Travis and his moronic friends. Brian was so stubborn and they were so immature. Why couldn't everyone be a lesbian?

She took her time in the empty bathroom but instead of returning to the theater, she headed to the foyer and sat on a bench facing a large James Bond movie cutout. While she couldn't have cared less about Double-O-Seven, she loved the Bond women, particularly Halle Berry.

"Hey."

She'd been so busy thinking of Halle emerging from the ocean in a bikini that she hadn't noticed Sonia approach.

"Hey."

"Can I sit with you?"

Pandy slid over and Sonia joined her.

Sonia bit her lip and looked down. "I'm sorry about what happened earlier. Travis can be a total jerk. Is your head okay?"

She nodded. "Yeah. Why aren't you in the theater?"

"I don't know."

"Why do you hang out with him? Is he your boyfriend?"

She shook her head. "I don't know. All my friends wanted us to date and it just kinda happened." She glanced at her as if to gain her approval. "Pretty stupid, huh?"

Pandy shrugged. "I think you should only hang out with people who make you feel good about yourself."

Sonia seemed to ponder this. Then she turned and asked, "Can I tell you something, Pandy?"

"Sure."

"I bet you'd be good to hang out with. I mean, I'll bet you're really loyal to your friends."

Sonia stared at the bench's dark blue fabric. Pandy didn't know what to say. She wasn't used to getting compliments. In fact only a few adults like Ms. Clark and Mrs. Strauss ever said anything nice to her. She shifted her pinky finger ever so slightly toward Sonia who met her halfway. Pandy couldn't believe that she was practically holding hands with the hottest eighth grade girl at Cedar Hills. As if she was worried Pandy would mistake the touch as an accident, Sonia wrapped their fingers together.

"Is this okay?" Sonia asked softly.

"This is great," she replied, grinning. "I had no idea you were like me."

Sonia smiled. "Do you think we could hang out this weekend?"

"Yeah, sure." Her smile faded when she remembered the movie. "Sonia, can I ask you a personal question?"

"What?"

"When we go back inside are you gonna make out with Travis?"

Her cheeks reddened and she hung her head. "I don't know. I guess so. It's just a BJ. No big deal."

She couldn't believe it. "But it is a big deal, especially if you don't really like him that way. Then it's wrong." Sonia pulled her hand away and Pandy's stomach knotted. She shouldn't have been so judgmental. "I'm sorry. I shouldn't have said that. It's none of my business."

Sonia stood up. "You're right. It's not. And if you think I'm some sort of slut then I don't think we could ever be friends."

She turned away and went back into the theater. Pandy tried not to cry, and like a movie, she desperately wished she could rewind the last minute. Shit. Sonia was probably unzipping Travis's pants right at that moment just to spite her. She sighed deeply and decided to check on Brian. Maybe he'd be ready to go. The movie was only half over but she wanted to leave before Travis and his friends. And there was no way she could stay in the theater with Sonia sitting in the back pretending she was straight.

"Where have you been?" Brian hissed when she returned.

She noticed her seat and the floor around them were littered with small candies. She wiped off the seat before she sat down, careful not to look back toward Sonia and Travis. "How's the movie?"

"I wouldn't know. Those assholes ran out of candy about ten minutes ago and now they're throwing ice."

She gazed at him with pleading eyes. Brian hated to give up. "Let's just go. Please?"

He didn't answer. She noticed his fists were clenched and his body was tense.

"Are you okay?"

He shook his head. "No, I'm not. I'm so fucking sick of

those bastards." Then he turned to her and flashed a toothy grin. "I've got an idea. You get out of here and I'll meet you at the bus stop."

She looked at him suspiciously. "What are you going to do?"

"Don't worry about it. Now, go. And whatever you do, don't hang around. If I'm not there just get on the bus. It means I've gone to find Merrill. Okay?"

She hesitated. She knew she shouldn't leave him. He was going to get into trouble.

"Go," he repeated.

She moved to the steps and her gaze darted toward the corner. A daylight scene filled the movie screen and she watched Travis grab Sonia's head and attempt to push it toward his crotch. She was about to storm up the stairs when screams erupted. Brian charged across the wide row, passing all of Travis's friends and dumping the extra large soda across their laps. He disappeared through an exit near the screen and they jumped up and ran after him, Travis joining the chase.

Pandy stared at Sonia alone in the back row. Ushers appeared and the film was stopped. A group of adults surrounded the manager and started barking and pointing toward the wet seats. It was time to go. She ran to Sonia and took her hand.

"C'mon. Follow me."

They hustled out of the theater and walked the length of the mezzanine. Much to her relief they didn't trip over Brian's maimed and mutilated body.

"Where'd they go?" Sonia asked.

She shook her head. "I don't know. I should probably check the garage. You should go home." She dropped her hand and started for the stairs but Sonia followed behind.

"I'm coming with you. If they've caught Brian I might be able to talk to Travis."

They headed down to the first level and ascended the ramps leading to the roof, checking between the parked cars. Pandy was most worried about the corners of the garage where drug dealers hid and gang beatings regularly occurred. The smell of trapped exhaust was overwhelming and she found it difficult to breathe. While she wanted to be alone with Sonia it was impossible to carry on a conversation since a line of cars continually snaked past them on their way to the exit and the roar of the engines bounced off the concrete walls.

They reached the roof and the outdoors. Pandy breathed deeply, sucking in the fresh air and staring into the night sky. Her head was pounding from the fall against the concrete and she felt queasy. Only a few cars were parked on this level and it was obvious they were alone.

"We should go back down."

Sonia took her hand and squeezed. "I'm sorry, Pandy."

She looked into her worried face. If anyone knew what Travis was capable of doing it was Sonia. They had reason to be afraid. She turned to the exit but Sonia didn't move. She pulled her close and wrapped her in an embrace.

"I'm scared for Brian but I need to do this," she whispered.

The smell of strawberry filled Pandy's senses and her entire body tingled. No girl had ever hugged her like this. She felt wonderful and she just seemed to fit.

"I want you to know that I didn't make out with Travis and Brian's timing was really good."

Pandy looked into her eyes and nodded. "I know. I saw Travis trying to force you to go down on him. If Brian hadn't caused a scene I would have."

Sonia smiled and Pandy thought she was blushing. "Really?"

"Yeah. That wasn't gonna happen."

Sonia's beautiful blue eyes stared into hers. "Pandy, what you said in the lobby made me think. I mean, I really like you a lot."

Before she could say anything, Sonia's lips were pressed against hers for a quick kiss. It happened so fast she could barely enjoy it and then Sonia immediately backed away.

"I can't believe I did that."

"I'm glad you did."

The sound of Kelly Clarkson's *Breakaway* suddenly pierced the quiet of the night and she jumped. Sonia pulled her cell phone from her purse and checked the display. "It's Travis," she said before she answered. She held the phone out and they both listened.

"Where are you?" she said to him.

"Where the hell are you? I'm in front of the theater with my boys."

"I, um, headed to the parking garage to look for you. What happened?"

"What happened was we gave that little fuckin' faggot everything he deserved."

Pandy could hear laughter in the background. She put her hand over the phone and whispered in Sonia's ear. "Ask him where Brian is."

"So, where'd you guys leave him? You didn't beat him up where everybody could see, did you?"

"Don't worry about it. We chased him behind that seafood restaurant. There wasn't anyone around."

Pandy nodded. She knew where he was.

"I've gotta go. I called my mom and she's coming to pick me up so I'll see you at school."

Travis snorted. "Wait, don't you want to hang out some more?"

"No, I can't. I see my mom. 'Bye."

Sonia hung up and they raced down the four flights of stairs to the ground level. McCormick and Schmick's Seafood Restaurant sat at the far end of the Commons complex. Brian must have bolted down the escalator and run past the shops and buildings hoping he'd see Merrill or another security guard. She craned her neck right and left as they passed the connecting commercial structures. She pictured him stumbling into a corner his face bruised and bloodied. It made her move faster.

"There's the restaurant," Sonia said, pointing at a green awning that overlooked a curved driveway.

When they reached the edge of the building, Pandy veered right and headed into the service alley. One light shone over the trash dumpster but several dark corners gave her the creeps. The smell of fish and garbage was overwhelming and a path of trash snaked from the Dumpster into the shadows. It looked oddly out of place.

"What's that?" she asked.

"I don't know."

They slowly walked past the Dumpster from the far side of the service drive just in case someone was lurking in the dark, waiting to attack them. The trash trail ended in a huge mound against a block fence. When it suddenly rustled, she recognized the outline of Brian's trench coat buried among the debris.

"Oh, God," she murmured.

Brian sat against the fence covered in half-eaten seafood, table scraps and discarded fish heads. At first she thought he was unconscious but when she bent down she realized he was whimpering and stunk of urine. The moonlight glowed over his mottled face and a purplish bruise covered his left cheek.

"Jesus," Sonia said, as she wiped away the trash that covered much of his body. "What the hell did they do?"

He frowned like a little boy and his lip quivered. Pandy could tell he was cold and his coat was soaked with a variety of liquids. His eyes pooled with tears but he didn't cry.

"Can you stand up?" she asked.

He didn't answer but stared toward the service door. He made no effort to rise and she imagined if they walked away and left him the busboys would eventually find him and call the police—and he wouldn't care.

She took his face between her hands forcing him to look at her. "Tell me what happened."

He cried and gasped for air as he tried to talk. Much of what he said was incoherent, interrupted by frequent sobs. The group had chased him into the alley, punched him in the face and slammed him against the wall. When he fell to the ground nearly unconscious, they'd stood over him, making comments about faggots and penises. He'd made several sarcastic remarks, fueling their anger. At Travis's suggestion each one urinated on him and they poured several bags of trash over him before they left.

"We should call the police on those assholes," Sonia said. She pulled out her cell phone but Pandy touched her arm.

"Don't. It will only make it worse."

Sonia gasped. "Pandy, this is a hate crime. This is the stuff the teachers talked about during our unit on tolerance. The police need to be informed and the guys need to be arrested!"

"No," he whispered. "Listen to Pandy. There is no justice." He snorted. "Tolerance unit. Yeah, right."

She stared at Pandy and threw up her arms. "What is he talking about? What are *you* talking about?"

Pandy realized Sonia couldn't understand the situation. She'd never been an outcast. Prejudice was something she heard teachers preach about in class but she'd never lived with it. She was on the other side, the safe side, at least for now. As much as Pandy wanted to be with her, Sonia needed to be aware of the risks and the consequences for acting on her feelings.

"The police aren't going to do anything," Pandy explained. "They'll go to the guys' houses and take statements. Travis and his buddies will deny they did anything and it will be Brian's word against them—the Goth gay kid against the entire basketball team who happen to be part of National Junior Honor Society and have great GPAs. They'll get off but then they'll go after him again."

She watched Sonia process the information and her expression shifted from anger to exasperation.

"So you're saying if he tells they'll just look for another chance to get him."

She nodded. "That's how it works. It's just a circle. We need to take him home and let it go. He's probably safe for a while now. Maybe we'll get through the rest of the year without anything else happening."

"This is such BS!" Sonia yelled.

Brian took Pandy's hand and stood up. He practically fell over but righted himself against the Dumpster. "Just give me a sec," he mumbled.

"He can't get on the bus like this," Sonia said to her. "Should I call my mom? Or your mom?"

She realized how little Sonia knew about her. Maybe after she heard her story she wouldn't want to hang out. She pushed the thought away and just shook her head. "No, we shouldn't call any parents but you're right. They won't let him on the bus like this."

She debated what to do. There was only one person who would understand. She pulled out her cell phone and scrolled through her list of contacts.

Fifteen minutes later Ms. Clark's beat-up Honda pulled into the service alley. She'd brought a large garbage bag for the trench coat and one of her boyfriend's T-shirts so the ride home would be bearable. She said very little except to ask for directions to Brian's house. They pulled up to the curb, Ms. Clark intent on talking to his parents, until they realized his parents were out. They watched him trudge through the side gate and out of sight carrying the garbage bag like Santa's gift sack. Ms. Clark faced them and glanced at their entwined fingers.

"Pandy, what do you think I should do about tonight?"

"Nothing."

"I disagree. Do you know who did this?"

"No," she lied.

Ms. Clark stared at her for a long time. "Is this over?" she finally asked.

Pandy nodded. "Yes."

"Are you sure?"

"I think so."

"We'll discuss this further but we've said enough for now," Ms. Clark concluded, starting her car. She turned up the radio and U2 burst from the speakers.

Sonia whispered in Pandy's ear. "I understand what you were trying to tell me earlier. I've learned a lot tonight."

Pandy squeezed her hand and moved closer. "I'm glad you get it."

"But it's not over. Those guys need to pay for what they did."

She saw the fire in Sonia's eyes. She didn't think the president of the student council, who happened to be the nicest girl in the eighth grade, was capable of such a look. It made her shiver.

Chapter Fifteen

Faye awoke with a pounding headache, the result of too many tequila shots at Jonnie's birthday party. After pressing the snooze button for the third time she opened one eye and willed herself to sit up. Usually she could be coaxed out of bed but her motivation hinged on Andi's insistence that they start the day with a quick trip to the gym. When she was alone at her place she couldn't find the desire even with a map. She blinked three times and rubbed her temples. She wished Andi were here but she had to meet Marjorie at six fifteen for a breakfast strategy meeting and had insisted on staying at her place alone. Then Faye could sleep in her own bed and not be disturbed when Andi woke up early to primp.

She only worried for a split-second that Marjorie would say something to Andi about their relationship but she doubted it.

For the two months since their cruise no one in the district had mentioned it. Faye was grateful since she'd yet to muster enough courage to tell Andi they'd been found out.

She shuffled to the kitchen in search of coffee and the bottle of aspirin. The evening had been fun and enlightening. It was official. Jonnie was dating Rob. Faye was still accepting that fact and she'd been surprised when he'd pulled Jonnie into his arms and kissed her passionately while they waited for a table. It was weird seeing her professional and personal lives collide.

"It's new for them," Andi whispered in her ear. "And please wipe that look of revulsion off your face."

They'd gone to Switch, a great gay bistro that was far enough away from the school district boundaries to ensure that no one would accidentally wander by and watch them suck limes or each other's faces, which Jonnie and Rob continued to do throughout the evening.

They reveled in winter's demise and paid homage to spring by retiring their jackets and long-sleeved shirts. For Jonnie it was a tradition. Her May first birthday meant the celebration of impending summer and she looked great in Capri pants and a pink tank top that made Rob's tongue wag. The tray of tequila shots peeled away their inhibitions and soon other patrons were craning their necks toward them as their laughter grew into shrill cackles. Everything was funny and they were having a blast.

"Elise has asked that we don't make a big production out of her birthday," Rob announced.

Faye snorted. "Fat chance. Did you tell her we've got it planned already?"

"No, I didn't say anything. I just hope she doesn't have heart failure when she finds out about you."

She smirked. "I'm not sure coming out on her birthday is such a good idea. That may not be a great time."

"It's never a good time," Rob argued. "You've always got an excuse. Christmas is too busy, Easter is too religious, Arbor Day is too—"

"Stop," she said, pointing at him.

"Why doesn't she want a party?" Jonnie asked.

Faye laughed. "Sweetie, you're young. You're only thirty-one now. It's difficult to understand what it must be like to be *half a century* old."

Jonnie shrugged and drained her shot. "I believe you're as old as you feel." She turned to Rob and grabbed his tie, pulling his mouth to hers for a sizzling kiss. "How old do you feel, baby?"

Faye leaned over the table. "Yes, Rob, tell us how you feel?"

Her brother turned crimson and glanced at them. He paused before he said, "Considering I'm the only male here surrounded by three beautiful women in a *gay friendly restaurant*, I'm feeling pretty damn good." His shit-eating grin made the women roar.

"I'm surprised you wanted to come here, Jonnie. I didn't know you knew about this place," Andi said.

Jonnie glanced at Rob and bit her lip before replying. "The fact is, Andi, I used to bring my girlfriend here."

Faye's jaw dropped. "You had a girlfriend?"

"*Used* to have a girlfriend," Jonnie emphasized. "I'm only dating Rob now."

"Still, you're bi?"

She glanced again at Rob, whose expression was neutral. Faye guessed this was covered ground and he didn't have a problem with it. "Yeah, I guess you'd say I'm bisexual. I've been with men and women. I have no preference about the sex of a person, but..." She gently caressed Rob's cheek and he smiled at her. "I do care who that person is, what he or she stands for."

Faye imagined that Jonnie had found a kindred spirit in Rob. The back of her car was covered with bumper stickers supporting Democratic candidates and various social causes while his truck was plastered with slogans that supported free thought. She could picture the two of them sitting up until the wee hours of the morning discussing global warming and bashing George W. Bush.

"Well," Andi drawled, "I think ya'll are cuter than a box of puppies." She wrapped her arm around Faye. "What do you say, babe? Look at 'em. They're waiting for your approval."

She stared at the couple realizing how much she loved them both. It would be great if it could work. She flagged down the waitress. "Could we get a bottle of champagne?"

When the plant foreman greeted Faye at the school's front door an hour later, she sensed the day had begun without her. He nervously bounced from one foot to the other as she approached.

"What's wrong, Del?" she asked, walking past him toward her office.

"We've got a problem. Over the weekend the mural was tagged."

"Shit."

She dropped her briefcase on her desk, grabbed the digital camera and followed him out to the amphitheater. She could see the black, angular letters from a distance—SSL—the customary tag for the Sixteenth Street Locos. Underneath were the words, *Fucking Faggots*, only Faggots was spelled with one g.

"Damn gangs," she said.

She glanced at her watch. Students would be arriving in ten minutes and the profanity would need to be removed immediately before a small child added it to his dinnertime vocabulary.

"Get some paint," she said sharply and Del hurried to his workshop while she snapped pictures for the police.

"What happened, Ms. Burton?"

A second grader named Lulu approached and Faye stepped in front of her, making a mental note to call her mother about the official arrival time. She directed her to the library as Del returned with some supplies and a can of maroon paint that he used to touch up the basketball floor.

"At least it's one of our school colors," she said.

Del quickly dumped the paint into a pan and rolled the wall, beginning with the slur. *Fucking faggots* quickly disappeared and she sighed with relief. He continued to cover the mural, violating the students' work with vicious, haphazard streaks. It seemed worse than the graffiti. She turned away and headed back to the office. There would need to be a statement on morning announcements about the mural and she wanted to offer a reward for information about the vandal.

Jonnie was devastated when she learned what had happened and she pulled Pandy out of class to tell her. Ruby Taylor wanted someone's head on a stick and the other art students were outraged. Faye thought there was a decent chance they'd find the vandal since so many students had helped make the mural a reality.

An hour later, Pete strolled into her office. "Hey, I think we've got our artists. It's Poncho and Turtle. They're not very bright. A student heard Turtle bragging about it at Starbucks this morning."

"Are they here?"

"Yep. They're in my office but they're not talking. They know the drill. Never admit to anything. They know confession is bullshit and you should *never* tell the truth."

"I hope you don't give that speech to the other kids," she said dryly. "Which of our vandals is easier to break?"

"Turtle."

"Bring him in."

While Pete went to claim Turtle she grabbed another cup of coffee from the lounge. Jonnie hurried by and headed toward the refrigerator. "I hear Turtle and Poncho are the ones."

"Yeah. Somebody heard them bragging but they're not owning up. I really want them to confess. It would make everything so much easier." She rubbed her left shoulder; a ball of tension nestled underneath the blade.

She glanced at Jonnie who was shaking a bottle of juice and seemed to want to say something. "Faye, are you really cool with me and Rob?"

"Yeah, I am. And the more I think about it the more I realize that I should have set you guys up a long time ago. Just promise me you won't break his heart and you'll be gentle with him."

Jonnie raised an eyebrow. "How gentle?"

Faye scowled. "Too much information."

Jonnie giggled, gave Faye's throbbing shoulder a quick squeeze and ran out.

She took a few sips of coffee and stared out the window. There wasn't any hurry and it was good to let Turtle stew for a few minutes.

The bell rang and she watched the courtyard fill with students passing to their next class. It was a three-minute reminder of the joys of youth. They laughed unabashedly at their friends' jokes and wore the blithe expressions that only children could muster for a significant length of time. She knew that many of them carried enormous baggage and endured horrible private lives but here they found security, an opportunity for the future and the chance to be a child if only for seven hours a day. Students like Turtle and Poncho jeopardized that slice of hope.

She returned to her office and slammed the door shut. Turtle whipped his head to the side. He was a typical gangbanger dressed in a SouthPole T-shirt and baggy Dickies pants. He had a very round face and his eyebrow was shaved, another sign of gang membership. He wore an indifferent expression as if someone accustomed to the inside of the principal's office, but he played with his shirttail nervously. Faye saw a sliver of possibility but it meant she had to play tough.

She went to the bookshelf and retrieved the large notebook of governing board policies. When she dropped it on her desk, Turtle jumped suddenly. She didn't bother to look at him and thumbed through the sections until she found the passage she wanted.

Her finger dramatically trailed across the page as she read. "Students who engage in gang behavior will face serious disciplinary consequences which may include long-term suspension, alternative placement or expulsion." Only then did she jerk her head up to check his expression. Nothing.

"Do you know what all that means, Guillermo?" His head twitched slightly and he remained mute. "It means that if people lie to me about what happened to the mural I can have them thrown out of school. I could also file police charges against them as well. Somebody's gonna be in deep shit. Do you understand?"

He nodded slightly.

"What do you know?"

He shrugged. "Nothing."

His response was automatic. It was just as Pete had said. The threat of police intervention and her use of profanity would break most students, the truth tumbling from their lips. But Turtle was hard core and those kids never broke, never snitched and never cared about adults. For a fleeting moment she thought of the difference twenty years made. Her generation packed up honesty and integrity and took them to college. Those were foreign concepts to Turtle and his crew.

"You don't know anything," she said, debating how far she wanted to push ethical boundaries. They stared at each other until he blinked.

"No."

"You don't care if I call the police."

"No."

"You don't care if I expel you."

"I don't know nothing," he whispered, avoiding the question.

She conveniently forgot that the gang member sitting across from her was thirteen years old.

"Guillermo, you need to listen very carefully," she said softly, in a voice barely above a whisper. "I'm extremely angry right now about what has happened to our school. I'm going to catch whoever did this and he's going to pay. And anyone who lies to me is going to pay extra. I hate liars. And if I have to spend another hour on this someone's going to leave this school in handcuffs and get a trip to jail. Do you know what they do to people in jail?"

"No, but my uncle's in jail." It was the longest answer he'd offered. He shifted in his seat and blinked his eyes.

"Someone could go to jail for this and I'm beginning to think that someone should be you. I don't think you'll like jail. You know what happens to boys in jail? They get girlfriends named Frank. Do you know what I'm saying to you, Guillermo?"

He swallowed hard and she thought she saw the hardness in his eyes soften slightly.

"Do you like boys, G?"

His eyes grew wide and his lips trembled. He shook his head.

"You don't want a boyfriend?"

"No," he mouthed, but no real words came out.

"Who sprayed the mural?"

"Me and Poncho."

She smiled. "Thank you. Go back to Mr. Salinas's office and don't talk to Poncho."

He wiped some tears from his eyes but years of experience told her that these were not tears of remorse, but fear—not of her—but of his homies, probably Carlos, the leader, who would undoubtedly jump him once he learned Turtle had snitched. He bolted out the door and she sighed heavily.

Turtle was afraid of Carlos but he was more afraid of homosexuality. She'd played to his greatest fear—his prejudice— and in her effort to solicit his confession, she'd validated that fear for the greater good. But it still didn't sit well with her.

A scream tore through the hallway and A.J. bounded around the corner, Coach Fleming chugging behind. Faye jumped from her chair and met Pete and Jonnie in the hallway. The four adults formed a circle around A.J. who paced liked a caged animal trying to get by.

"What happened?"

Coach noticed Poncho sitting a few feet away and pulled the adults to the side. "A.J. grabbed Jenny Kottmer by the hair and tried to kiss her."

Faye shook her head, mortified. "Is Jenny okay?"

"She's being examined by Nurse Chang. She's pretty shaken up."

Faye gazed down at A.J. He'd plopped onto the floor and the screams deflated into panting sounds. Poncho watched, clearly stunned by his peer's behavior.

Pete sighed loudly. "So much for P.E. What do we do with him now?"

They agreed there would need to be an investigation and depending on the reaction from Jenny's parents, there could be legal involvement. She knew that Steve and Sandy Kottmer had expressed concern about A.J.'s presence in the P.E. class and she doubted they would be very understanding. Bill Gleeson is a moron, she thought.

"I'll go and call Constance Richardson after I check on Jenny and contact her parents. Coach, you get back to class, and Pete, you keep an eye on A.J."

They looked down at him, his frail little body lying on the floor, studying the pattern in the carpet, and Poncho—the dangerous gangbanger. He'd pushed his chair against the wall, as far away from A.J. as possible, his eyes wide in amazement.

She pointed her finger at him. "Anybody need to watch you, Poncho?"

He raised his hands in surrender. "I'm good."

Chapter Sixteen

A slight breeze rustled the trees along the Tropics Trail and Constance smiled as the wind caressed her face. The unbearable summer weather was a few weeks away and every Arizonan would seize the remaining pleasant outdoor opportunities by crowding the parks, lakes and attractions. She'd taken Armour to the Phoenix Zoo and if this had been a weekend, the paths would be packed with families and strollers. Yet because it was a Thursday morning the zoo was practically deserted as they meandered past the elephant and the jaguar.

"Turtles, Mommy!" he cried, and ran on ahead toward the Galapagos turtle exhibit.

She almost called for him to wait but then she realized he wasn't in danger. They were alone and she could savor the distance between them. Going to the zoo was one of his favorite activities and she didn't mind taking him when it wasn't crowded. It was much safer than a park where children constantly threw sand at each other and made horrible shrieking sounds when they didn't get their way.

All of the commotion was too much stimulation for him. He would inevitably wind up in a corner wailing or he'd explode and slug a child. The last park visit cost Constance two hundred dollars to placate an angry parent whose bleeding child said Armour had hit her in the head with a tree branch. The zoo was much safer with glass, walls and metal bars separating him from the other animals.

They were stuck together today while he served his ridiculous one-day suspension for physical aggression, to use Faye Burton's terminology. No amount of money could persuade Cathy to skip the university classes she attended while he was at school and no reputable daycare center would take him. He'd either been kicked out or they didn't take disabled children. Constance had no choice but to accept her motherly role and lose twelve billable hours, something she hadn't done in three years.

She watched him run, his body moving sideways almost as often as forward. He looked like a penguin, tilting back-and-forth as he approached the brick wall that formed the circular enclosure. He climbed on a rock to peer inside and sat perfectly still. She knew he would remain frozen for a while since the turtles were his favorite. She wondered if he felt some sort of kinship with the odd-looking, slow-moving beasts.

She settled on a nearby bench and took out her BlackBerry, prepared to answer a few e-mails and send some text messages but she found herself taken by the serenity of the scene. It was very quiet and the sun warmed her face. It reminded her of a Kansas spring and Cora.

When their mother died a month before Constance's eleventh birthday, Cora immediately assumed the maternal role, caring for her and making sure she ate her vegetables and did her homework. Cora never abandoned her and they were always best friends despite the slew of male suitors who desperately wanted to make time with Cora. While Constance was brilliant and bookish, Cora turned heads whenever she smiled. She didn't care for school and it was only her empathetic teachers who ensured she walked across the stage at high school graduation.

Constance thought Cora would have her suitcase packed the next day and take the bus out of Atwood, but she remained, working in a diner and caring for her and their father. Always somewhat selfish, Constance didn't think about her motivations. She was just glad that Cora remained in her life, a buffer between her and their father who had turned into an entirely different person after their mother's death.

On the night Constance graduated from high school, the two of them sat up in the tree house, smoking a joint and giggling hysterically.

"When are we going to Hollywood?" Constance asked.

Cora, who was twenty-two, passed her the joint and shrugged. "I don't know. We'll see."

It was the last time they ever discussed it. Although Constance was buzzed from the pot, she heard a different tone in Cora's voice. The words suggested hope but they lacked conviction. She sounded nothing like the starstruck girl who once used the tree house as her stage. Looking at her, she saw the weariness in Cora's eyes, fatigue from carrying a dying dream. She realized then that her sister would never leave Atwood.

"Mommy! Let's go see the monkeys," Armour said, jumping up and down in front of her.

She offered a relieved smile, grateful for the interruption. She'd spent far too much time wallowing in the past. She tossed her BlackBerry into her bag and followed him down the path toward the monkey compound. He constantly veered off the path, climbing over every rock and traipsing through much of the surrounding foliage. At least he'd stopped trying to scale the animal enclosures.

At these moments Constance truly understood what a maniac Armour must be at school. She was tired after only a few hours and she couldn't imagine how hard it was for Mrs. Strauss to get through the day. But that wasn't her problem. Mrs. Strauss had chosen her profession and dealing with Armour was part of her contract.

And she was furious with Faye Burton, the spiteful bitch. She was certain the suspension was retaliation for forcing the P.E. issue, which she'd thought was going quite smoothly after a month.

There only had been two minor incidences where Armour hit another student with a ball—but only because he was excited. He hadn't been suspended for those. What's a couple bloody noses? But she knew Faye Burton had been waiting for this moment, hoping Armour would fail to control himself. She'd seen Burton smile when she'd escorted Armour from the office, his screams gaining the attention of everyone in the lobby. It was clear to her that Faye and Pete Salinas *enjoyed* suspending her son and they deliberately pressed his buttons to exacerbate his poor behavior. How dare Faye Burton humiliate her in public? It'd taken all of her restraint not to denounce Burton as a lesbian right then and there. She wanted to scream in her face that she knew her secret and she could ruin her career.

But she'd quickly deduced it wasn't the right time. The effect would be lost in the chaos Armour created and she didn't have the proper audience. Most likely that slob Salinas and many of the teachers already knew about Burton. She certainly telegraphed her lesbianism. No, Constance needed to exercise patience just as she did in court, waiting for the precise moment to discredit a witness or topple her opponent's case. She smiled at the thought of Bill Gleeson learning that one of his principals—whose school was filled with stuffy, uptight Republicans—was a dyke.

When she finally caught up to Armour, he was standing in front of the glass, facing a chimp. The beast reached up to scratch his head and he did the same. The monkey scratched his armpit and he followed suit. She was amused until he stuck his index finger in his nose and the chimp ran away.

He roared, "Fasty native!"

Chapter Seventeen

Faye knew an ambush when she saw one. At the end of their monthly administrators' meeting Marjorie had quickly approached her before she could leave and asked her to come into the superintendent's office. Faye glanced at Andi who shook her head. She had no idea what was going on. She'd barely sat down in the plush conference room chair when Gleeson began.

"Please update me on A.J. Richardson's progress. How is he doing in P.E.?"

Horribly, she thought. Coach Fleming complained about A.J.'s behavior on a daily basis.

Faye chose her words carefully, remembering that A.J.'s placement was Gleeson's idea and the upside of appeasing Constance had been the departure of the state auditor from Andi's life.

"I know you're aware he was already suspended once for pulling a girl's hair."

Gleeson frowned, his pen scratching the notepad. "Was that really necessary?"

"Well, he tried to kiss her," Faye added, shocked that she was being questioned.

"Ms. Burton, I do hope you're not letting your personal dislike of Ms. Richardson affect your judgment."

Marjorie's hand touched her arm and Faye swallowed the profanity-laden retort that had nearly escaped her lips. Then Marjorie offered a preparatory cough, as if she was letting Gleeson know she was about to speak.

"Bill, I know you haven't worked with Faye for long, but I assure you that she is the epitome of fairness with students and parents."

Faye knew that Marjorie was trying to help but she also knew the support was fleeting and Dr. Marshmallow would abandon Faye's life raft the minute Gleeson suggested she do so.

He studied both of them while he tapped the paper. "Keep me apprised," he concluded.

She started to push away from the conference table when he said, "Now, this mural business."

He placed the gold pen precisely at the top of the tablet and folded his hands in front of him.

To have enough time to worry about how I set my pen down, she thought.

Faye glanced at Marjorie and imagined she spent at least an hour in front of the mirror each morning, but her entire makeup case couldn't hide the worry lines crossing her face. Wherever this was going it wasn't good.

"Ms. Burton, both Dr. Machabell and I have fielded several complaints from concerned parents *and* teachers over the content of your mural."

"Can you outline those complaints for me specifically?"

Gleeson sighed, apparently perturbed. "It's too controversial. Including religion and gay rights in artwork that sits on a *public* school campus..." He paused and shook his head. "It shows incredibly poor judgment on your part but your judgment is a discussion for another day. These vandals have, in my opinion, done us a favor. We're not going to make the same mistake twice. I don't want it redone at least not with that design. You'll need to pick something that is less controversial."

"Less controversial," she repeated, stunned.

He nodded.

"You wouldn't have any suggestions, would you?"

"No," was the stony reply.

She drummed the table and turned to Marjorie. "What about some flowers?"

"That might be lovely," Marjorie said with a smile, oblivious to her sarcasm.

She shook her head. "No, on second thought, that's too girlie. It'll offend the boys." She snapped her fingers. "I know. We could do a celebration of books." She looked from Gleeson, whose temper was clearly rising, to Marjorie, who was entirely uncomfortable and probably wanted to put a hand over her mouth.

"No, I take that back," she said. "People would probably complain about the titles we chose. You know, all those nasty books that make kids think. Hmm. What could we do? Ah, a design of the Milky Way galaxy, a celebration of planets. That's it." She looked at Gleeson. "Was there anything else?"

"No."

She started to leave and turned around. "Oh, darn. We can't do a celebration of the planets." She faked a frown and shook her head. "It might offend the extraterrestrials."

She left before either of them could comment. She'd just written the script for her own dismissal and she suddenly dreaded her evaluation which was slated to occur in less than a month, right before her summer vacation—if she still had a job.

She automatically headed up the stairs to Andi's office, realizing that the world was exploding around her. She owed it to Andi to let her know the truth.

She heard her familiar laugh through the open door and saw she was on the phone. Faye nodded at Estella before closing the door behind her.

Andi saw her expression and said, "I gotta go." She hung up and looked at her with concern. "Babe, what's wrong?"

She took a deep breath, unsure of where to start. "I think you need to know a few things. First, Bill Gleeson is a homophobic bastard."

Andi snorted and leaned back in her chair. "Okay, what else?"

"Marjorie Machabell is a fucking hypocrite."

"What do you mean?"

"Honey, she knows about us."

Andi gripped the sides of her chair. "What do you mean Marjorie knows about *us*?"

She shrugged and perched on the edge of Andi's desk. "She must have seen us at that board meeting and I think she grilled Estella for more details."

"What?"

"I'm sorry, babe."

The wheels in Andi's mind were clearly turning and she slowly shook her head. "Jesus, I can't believe this. Oh, my God. What about Gleeson?"

"Well, I think he's clueless and I'm rather certain this is my last year in the district—"

"But what about me? Does Gleeson know about me?"

Andi's charge toward self-preservation disarmed Faye momentarily. "No, honey, I don't think he does. Thanks for your support, though," she added sarcastically.

Andi slumped in her chair and covered her face. "Honey, I'm sorry if I sound selfish but you've made your choices and I've made mine."

"And you've chosen to hide."

Andi pointed, ready for a fight when a quick knock drew their attention to the door and Estella peered inside. "Sorry to interrupt but I got a phone call from Pete, Faye. You need to get back to school and he said Andi should come too. Apparently A.J. Richardson had a meltdown."

"Crap," she said. "Did Pete say what happened?"

"No, but it must be pretty bad. He told me to tell you the police are on their way."

The conversation resumed once they were safely cloistered inside Faye's truck for the two-mile drive to Cedar Hills.

"I'm not hiding," Andi said emphatically. "I'm just a private person, Faye. The world is filled with people who have given up every ounce of their dignity. It's okay to talk about anything with anyone at *any* time. There's no decorum left in the world. The way I was raised you kept things to yourself and nobody talked about religion, politics or sex in public."

Thoughts of Andi's parents wandered into her head but she knew to mention them would send her over the edge.

"I don't want to talk about this now," she said quietly. "I'm sorry I ever brought it up, Texas."

"Well I'm not, if that's how you really feel." Andi's drawl was thick and Faye could tell she'd not only struck a nerve, she'd severed a major artery.

She sighed heavily. "Honey, I'm just upset. Gleeson's out to get me, the mural's been destroyed and only a week after dealing with Constance Richardson and A.J.'s last suspension, I'm going to get the pleasure of meeting with her again. If Pete called the police, A.J.'s going to be suspended and she'll probably refile her complaint with the state and make more problems for you."

She glanced at Andi. The anger was gone and she could tell Andi had shifted into her professional role. She met her gaze and offered a sympathetic smile.

"We're not done talking about this but I'll let it go for now, okay?"

They pulled into the parking lot and saw the police cruiser at the front door. She realized the office was different the moment she opened the door. The lobby was empty and the only sound was the receptionist's ringing phone.

"Where is everyone?" Andi asked.

"I don't know."

They headed down the hallway toward Faye's office and saw something lying on the floor. It was a boy's shirt. She picked it up and looked at Andi, who was already shaking her head. They passed her office, and Pete's and Jonnie's—all vacant—but they came upon a pair of pants, socks, shoes and finally underwear as they turned the corner.

Hushed voices floated from the end of the hallway—the office kitchen. Sitting at the small table where they all regularly ate lunch was Pete, his chin resting on his upheld palm, watching Nurse Chang, who was down on one knee, talking sweetly to A.J. while she bandaged his bloody left hand. The large muscular arms of a Phoenix police officer were wrapped around A.J.'s naked chest, holding him still. A box of cereal sat on the table between the two men.

"Oh, God," Andi murmured into Faye's ear.

Pete quickly joined them in the corridor and said, "He attacked Jenny Kottmer in P.E. Gave her a titty twister."

"A what?" Andi asked.

"It's when a boy grabs a girl's breast and twists," Faye explained. "Where's Jenny?"

"She's in Chang's office with Jonnie. She's crying and really shaken up. Apparently it happened when Coach Fleming was lining up the kids. She called me immediately and Jonnie and I went down there to help Jenny and remove A.J., who started screaming when I told him he had to leave. I practically had to carry him back to the office. When I set him down in a chair and went to close the door, he jumped up and ran out before I could stop him."

Pete took a breath and raked his hand through his disheveled hair. He was rattled and his hands were shaking. "He ran through the hallways screaming fasty native and he started pulling off his clothes. I couldn't catch him so I told Marian to get everyone out of the office. The kids didn't need to see that. And then he ran into the kitchen. Somebody left a paring knife on the counter and he grabbed it by the blade end."

"Shit," Faye said. "Is he all right?"

Pete nodded and Faye could see the tears in his eyes. "He wouldn't drop it. I stood in the doorway and tried to calm him down. I knew if he started to run again he'd probably stab himself. Marian called nine-one-one and Officer Friendly showed up. Thank God he's a big guy. We cornered A.J. but he wouldn't drop the knife. Then I remembered the box of cereal I'd brought in last week. It had a picture on the back of Mr. Zex."

"Who?" Andi asked.

"A.J.'s favorite cartoon character," Faye said.

"So we traded and he calmed down until Chang came to check him out. He tried to bolt again and the officer grabbed him. That's about when you walked in." Pete took another deep breath and shook his head. "I'm sorry, Faye. I should've known he'd run."

She shook her head. "You couldn't know this was going to happen. It's not your fault. He shouldn't even be here," she added, shooting a searing gaze at Andi who seemed lost in her own thoughts. Nurse Chang emerged from the kitchen holding several bloody gauze pads.

"He's given himself a rather deep cut on his palm and he should definitely be seen by a doctor. Have we called his mother?"

As if on cue, Constance Richardson barreled around the corner, clutching A.J.'s clothes. "What the hell have you people done with my son?" she barked.

"There's been an accident, Ms. Richardson," Faye began, but before she could explain, A.J. heard his mother's voice.

"Mommy!"

"What's happened?" she gasped at the sight of her naked son in the arms of a police officer with a huge bandage around his hand.

Faye moved next to her. "We need to sit down and talk—"

"Like hell! I'm taking my son to the emergency room right now!"

A.J. wriggled out of the officer's grasp and she dressed him while she continued to rant at Faye. "This school is filled with nothing but incompetents. I expect a full report explaining why my son is naked, the police are present and how he hurt himself."

"He ran away from Mr. Salinas—"

"I don't want your pathetic excuses, Ms. Burton! I'll be speaking to Superintendent Gleeson about this matter."

"Go right ahead," Faye said softly. "Jenny Kottmer's parents may choose to take legal action, an idea I'll encourage. If you won't do the right thing for your son, I'll force the issue."

"You know nothing about me or my son," she said, taking a now compliant A.J. by the hand and starting out the door.

"He's suspended for another five days," Faye called. "We'll contact you about the hearing."

She whirled around and faced Andi. "What hearing?"

Andi was the epitome of calm. "There will need to be a hearing, Ms. Richardson. This incident has clearly called the question about A.J.'s placement."

Constance's gaze shifted from Andi to Faye. "I guess I should've expected the two of you to be in bed together," she said and walked away.

Their attention drifted to Pete and the responding officer, but Faye watched Andi's expression crack in half at Constance Richardson's parting shot.

Chapter Eighteen

The bell chimed and Pandy scurried out the door. She wanted to be the first to leave and avoid the crowd in the hallway. Her fourth period Spanish teacher continued to shout information about their final exam, hoping to be heard over the din of the exiting students. Pandy caught something about studying transitive verbs but she didn't really care. She could get a big fat *cero* on her final and still pass the class.

Shouts and whoops echoed throughout the corridors as more classes were released for the yearbook party. They all stampeded down the stairs toward the cafeteria. Rap music bellowed through some huge speakers and long tables full of food lined one side of the cafeteria. After she got her yearbook she settled in a corner with Brian and the rest of her lunch group so they could flip through the pages.

Brian said nothing. Since the incident at the Commons he was extremely quiet. He'd refused to talk about it with anyone, and when Ms. Clark had insisted on calling his parents, he'd paid a neighbor to pose as his father and sworn Pandy to secrecy. Pandy hated to lie to Ms. Clark but she'd promised him.

Pandy knew that she would be featured once in the yearbook—her class picture. Only the A-list would be remembered multiple times, enjoying their lunch, playing sports or goofing off for the camera. They were popular and photogenic, the two required characteristics that guaranteed multiple page listings in the index. She grimaced at her terrible photo taken the morning after a bad cutting episode. She looked timid and sad and the graininess of the tiny black-and-white image was totally unappealing. She wondered what Sonia would think when she saw it.

No one knew they were seeing each other—except Brian—and they'd agreed to stay apart at school but Sonia had insisted they meet during the yearbook party. Pandy appreciated her status and didn't want to jeopardize her place on the social ladder. Instead they spent most of their evenings IMing and talking about their friends on MySpace. She was teaching Sonia about gay vocabulary and culture and Sonia was helping her deal with her fucked up life, as she liked to call it. Pandy had confessed much of her past in Utah, at least the edited version. She didn't think Sonia could handle the whole truth. She knew she couldn't.

When the clock finally hit one fifty-nine, she said to Brian, "I'm meeting Sonia in the ceramics court for a little while. I'll be back."

He nodded, still clutching his unopened yearbook.

She moved toward the exit door. Principal Burton was talking to the yearbook advisor. There were other adults chaperoning the event but they were all signing yearbooks. She slid out and strolled around the building. The gate to the ceramics court was open and she ducked inside the small shelter. Arms immediately wrapped her in an embrace and she started to laugh.

"Hey," Sonia whispered.

"Hi."

They held each other and didn't let go.

"Is this okay?" Sonia asked.

"Uh-huh."

"I don't know what else to do," Sonia said shyly.

Pandy grinned and leaned against the block wall. "Well, nothing here. We *are* at school."

They both laughed and Sonia looked away. Pandy thought she might be embarrassed but when Sonia held out her yearbook, she wore a perfect smile.

"Sign, please."

"Can we wait until this weekend? You know, when you come over? I want to write some stuff and it'll take some time."

Sonia blushed and nodded. "Yeah, that's a good idea." She took her hand. "What I want to say might take most of a page. Can you save me a spot?"

Pandy rolled her eyes. "Yeah, I'm pretty sure you can sign wherever you want." She looked down at their fingers, enjoying the connection. She couldn't explain it but she really liked touching Sonia. Somehow it just felt right. It felt important.

"Will there be any space left for me?" Pandy asked.

"Of course." Sonia rested her forehead against Pandy's. "You're really the only person I want to sign my book. I care about what you say."

Sonia kissed her first. When she felt Sonia's breasts against her own, she thought she might pass out. There was too much to think about—the kiss, their bodies touching and an incredible new feeling creeping between her legs. When they finally broke apart, they giggled. Pandy couldn't explain what was happening and she was afraid Sonia could tell.

"Um, that was really hot," Sonia said. "It felt really good."

"Yeah," Pandy agreed, trying to lift her eyes to meet Sonia's gaze. "You're a great kisser."

Sonia beamed. "So are you. I want to do it again."

They continued kissing and Pandy felt Sonia's tongue flick into her mouth. She'd never Frenched anyone but Sonia was obviously experienced.

"Holy shit!" a voice cried.

Travis and two of his buddies stood in the doorway. He

stared at Sonia, hardly noticing that Pandy was there.

"This is why you didn't want to go out with me anymore? Because you're a dyke? I can't believe it!" He turned to the two other boys, Sean, who'd helped beat up Brian, and Dylan, another basketball player. "Look at this, guys."

"I think that one turned your girlfriend into a lesbo," Sean said.

"She did not, asshole," Sonia replied. "Get the hell out of our way."

She grasped Pandy's arm and they attempted to pass Travis but he remained planted in the doorway.

"I don't think so. You and your girlfriend are gonna have to pay the fee."

"Move," Sonia snarled, trying to sound tough as she pushed against Travis. He shoved her hard and she fell onto the concrete floor.

"Sonia!" Pandy screamed.

"Grab her, Dylan," Travis instructed.

Dylan pulled Sonia from the floor and she cried out, cradling her right arm.

"Sean and I are gonna show little miss dyke what she's missing. She needs to pay for turning my girlfriend into a muff diver."

Sean and Travis advanced toward her and she flew around Ms. Taylor's workbench. They circled the bench from opposite sides, surrounding her.

"Travis, leave her alone," Sonia sobbed.

"Fuck, no," he said, playfully lunging toward Pandy and making kissing sounds. "I'm gonna find out if she likes boys."

Pandy took two steps backward and the heel of her right foot butted against something hard and immovable—the wall. She looked from Travis to Sonia, held tightly in Dylan's grip, and began to shake.

"I'm gonna show you what you're missing," Travis said.

In three steps he was against her. She screamed but a deep, primal cry echoed throughout the court.

"Fuck!" Sean shouted.

Brian stood in the doorway, a baseball bat in his hands, now covered with Dylan's blood. Dylan lay in a heap at Sonia's feet.

"Davies," Travis said, "Be cool, man."

Sonia darted out the door and Brian let her pass. His expression was an unreadable mask and he flicked the bat from one hand to the other with great dexterity. Pandy had seen him do that before—two years earlier when he'd played Little League. He was really good but he'd quit because of the taunts and endless slurs about being a gay boy.

He swung the bat fiercely, shattering a clay pot that sat on the workbench. It happened in an instant and Sean and Travis started babbling simultaneously, pleading with him to put the bat down.

"Brian, be cool, man! Please! Don't hurt me!" He dropped to the floor, begging.

He reminded Pandy of A.J. when he was most upset, inconsolable. He was making it easy for Brian, who raised the bat above his head.

Pandy stepped in front of Travis, blocking Brian's swing. "Brian, don't. It's not worth it."

She held his gaze, trying to pull him from his rage and hatred. She knew Travis wasn't just Travis—he was everyone who'd ever messed with Brian.

"Please," she whispered.

Voices floated into the room and Pandy glanced at the doorway, filled with adults—Ms. Burton, Mr. Salinas, Ms. Taylor and Ms. Clark, who stepped inside.

"Brian, I need you to put the bat down, and Pandy, sweetie, I need you to step back."

Pandy shook her head. She knew Ms. Clark wanted her out of the way. Ms. Taylor had pulled Sean out of the room and was motioning to Pandy but she shook her head again. Brian was her friend and she was certain he wouldn't hurt her.

Ms. Clark moved a few steps closer, careful to stay in Brian's peripheral vision. She slowly set her hands on the workbench so Brian could see them.

"Pandy, is there something you want to tell Brian?"

Pandy realized Ms. Clark needed her help. Brian wouldn't listen to adults—only her.

"Yeah," she said automatically, although she had no idea what to say next. What could she possibly say to get him to put down the bat? All she could think about was what would happen to him if he killed Travis. Then she thought about what *her* life would be like without him and a lump formed in her throat.

When she spoke, she didn't recognize her voice. "Remember that secret I told you? The one I've never said to anyone? If you go away who can I talk to? Who's going to help me, Brian? You're my best friend. We count on each other, you know? C'mon, he's really not worth it."

She pulled off the leather bracelets and held up her wrists in front of her face, showing him the long red gashes he'd seen so many times.

"Please, Brian. Help me."

He stared at her wrists and then slowly lowered the bat until it dropped from his hands and clattered to the floor. She rushed into his arms and held his frail body tightly. A familiar hand gently rubbed her back and she knew Ms. Clark was rubbing Brian's back too. It was her gesture of love and comfort and it always reminded Pandy of Mama at her best.

And when Ms. Clark whispered, "It's going to be okay," she heard Mama's voice.

Chapter Nineteen

Throngs of people gathered in Elise's living room but its size afforded such a crowd. Glancing about the McMansion Faye was pointedly reminded of the differences between their lives. The spaciousness of the floor plan, the vaulted ceilings and the original artwork announced her sister's station in life. Yet Faye admired the place, which was designed with interesting angles and huge expanses of glass that overlooked the pool and desert landscape. There was a commitment to environmental integrity that reminded her of her mother. Although Elise was daddy's girl, Faye was pleased to see that fragments of her mother's social conscience had penetrated the capitalistic genetics Elise had inherited from their father.

Mitch had insisted Elise would be most comfortable in her own home for her fiftieth birthday. He'd politely excused himself from the planning, offering the location and a guest list. When they'd met with him, Faye noticed he never stopped playing doctor. He only asked questions, took notes and nodded. It was typical Mitch. She'd known the man for over twenty-five years and she hadn't heard him string together ten sentences at the same time.

The party was underway, although the guest of honor hadn't arrived. Alec and Lindsay played host and hostess, greeting all of their parents' friends with the appropriate etiquette and small talk learned from years of proper breeding in upper-crust society. Lindsay, truly her mother's daughter, made a point of introducing Jonnie, Rob, Andi and Faye to all of Elise's co-workers and charity buddies.

"I was expecting a little more snobbery," Andi whispered.

Faye shook her head. "It's there. They're just trained to cover it. They took classes in humility."

Andi chuckled and slapped her arm. "Where's your sister? You don't think she bailed, do you?"

"No, she'll come. Her friends are here and there'll be hell to pay at next week's tennis match if she blows them off," she said sarcastically.

"Be nice," Andi warned. "Are you going to tell her tonight?"

Faye sighed. "I haven't decided."

"Knock, knock!" Elise exclaimed.

Applause swept through the room. Those closest to the door shook Mitch's hand and hugged Elise, who smiled effusively. When she saw Faye, she broke away from the crowd and went to her. They hugged and Elise kissed Andi on the cheek.

She surveyed the room and said, "I thought for sure the place would be covered in black crêpe paper."

Faye grinned. "We thought about that and then we decided on a theme party like trailer trash but we resisted that one."

Elise offered a withering look. "Thanks."

Andi pointed at the long table in the corner loaded with oddly wrapped presents. "Instead we went with a white elephant party."

"Lovely," she said, attempting a smile.

Rob and Jonnie joined them and Elise eyed her brother shrewdly. "What's up with the two of you?"

They exchanged glances and Rob said coyly, "Nothing. This is a great party, Elise."

"No, no. You're not changing the subject. There's something different but I just can't put my finger on it." She stared at Rob intently. "My God, your eyes are totally bloodshot. You've either been smoking weed or you need some sleep." She turned to Jonnie. "He always looked like a zombie after he pulled an all-nighter in school or he spent an afternoon with his friend, Simon, the pothead."

Jonnie laughed and wrapped her arms around Rob. "Well, he hasn't been smoking weed but we were up late last night." She buried her head into his neck and giggled.

"I don't need the details," Faye said.

Rob blushed and swallowed hard. "No, actually I guess you do. Jonnie and I flew to Las Vegas yesterday after school."

"Las Vegas?" Faye said. It only took a second to realize what her brother had done. "You got married?"

They both nodded and Jonnie said, "Faye, Elise, I'm your sister-in-law now. Isn't that great?"

She held up her left hand, revealing a simple gold band, and then she threw her arms around Faye and Andi.

Elise stared at Rob. "I can't believe it. Why would you do that?"

He shrugged. "We didn't want to wait. Jonnie had no desire for a big wedding and I've already been that route. We just wanted to be together, so we left at four, got married around midnight and spent a little time in the casino and the hotel before we flew back this morning."

Faye could tell by the way her brother stared at Jonnie that he'd finally met someone he loved, and judging from the look Jonnie returned, it was mutual.

Elise shook her head. "I just don't understand. You've only known each other a short while."

"You don't have to understand, Elise," he said. "It's not your business. It's my life."

"Did y'all get married by one of those Elvis impersonators?" Andi asked.

"No," Jonnie said. "I'm not really big on Elvis music.

We got handed this flyer by a guy on the strip and it was an advertisement for this little church—"

"You picked your church from a flyer?" Elise was dumbfounded. "Are you pregnant?"

Jonnie grinned and cradled Rob's face in her hands. "Not yet but we're trying."

"Yeah, Elise," he added. "If I don't spread my seed, who'll carry on the family name?" He kissed Jonnie deeply and Elise walked away.

"Well, she didn't take that very well," Andi said.

Faye snorted. "No surprise."

"Congratulations to both of you. I think this calls for a toast," Andi said.

A waiter passed by with draughts of champagne and they each took one. Faye cleared her throat and held up her glass. "I'm not very good with speeches but I just want to say I love you, and Jonnie, I hope you keep your own name or it'll get really confusing at school." They clinked glasses and sipped the expensive champagne.

"And good luck to you, too, sister," Rob quickly added. "I'm counting on you to make your own big announcement tonight, seeing as how I just broke the ice."

"And that's exactly why tonight's probably not a great choice to tell Elise that she really doesn't know me at all."

He wagged his index finger at her. "Oh, no, you're not getting out of this because of me. You need to tell her, Faye, especially now that Andi's in the picture."

The three of them looked at Andi and she nearly choked on her champagne. "What have I got to do with anything?"

"Faye adores you. You're the one even if she doesn't know it yet." He leaned over and pecked Andi on the cheek.

Faye was shocked and said nothing as Rob took Jonnie outside to explore the patio, pool and cabana.

Andi turned to her, an amused expression on her face. "So is your brother psychic or is there something we should talk about?"

There was plenty they *could* talk about, like all the reasons Faye loved her. Very little bothered Andi and she didn't sweat the small stuff but the past week had been filled with enormous problems like the Brian Davies incident, the looming black cloud that was A.J. Richardson's hearing and the revelation that Andi and Faye's relationship wasn't a secret.

Ever the pragmatist, Andi faced each problem one at a time. She'd been a rock for the last three days as Faye handled the media, the authorities and the Davies family. She'd been a wreck and Andi kept her going, despite her own responsibility of preparing for what would be the final showdown with Constance Richardson.

Embroiled in the school drama, it was difficult to find time to discuss their relationship, but Andi had realized after two days at work that no one treated her any differently than before. That seemed to provide the most comfort to her, knowing that her co-workers didn't care that she was a lesbian.

It bothered Faye that they still hadn't addressed the main issue which was Andi's fear that Bill Gleeson would learn the truth, but Faye figured that once she left the district, it would be a non-issue.

"I really need to kiss you," Faye said, glancing around at the other partygoers.

Andi winked. "What's stoppin' you, babe?"

A smile spread across her face. "C'mon. Follow me."

She led Andi down a back hallway that veered behind the kitchen. They passed several members of the catering staff bearing trays of stuffed mushrooms and canapés. She saw the door she was looking for—the entry to the wine cellar. She twisted the knob and noticed it was locked. Not surprising. Mitch didn't want the hired help handing out the really expensive stuff by accident. She typed Elise's birthday into the security keypad and heard a click.

They glanced at the walls lined with racks and bins, containing hundreds of bottles of foreign and domestic wines. An exquisite granite counter ran across the back wall, a glass carafe and a bottle of old French wine displayed prominently in the center. Undoubtedly this was one of Mitch's best bottles, deserving of a special place.

The chill in the room was pronounced. She noticed Andi

rubbing her arms to stay warm and her nipples hardening through her silk shirt.

"How cold is it in here?"

"Around fifty-five." She pulled Andi against her. "I'll keep you warm."

They kissed and groped each other until Andi stepped away. "How about some wine?"

Faye laughed and grabbed a bottle of California red from a rack and poured them each a glass.

"Are you okay about Jonnie and Rob? I mean, really?" Andi asked.

"Why does everyone keep asking me that? I'm totally cool with it and I bet she's pregnant before Christmas," she added.

"I wouldn't be surprised if she's pregnant before the end of the party," Andi drawled.

They both laughed and enjoyed the solitude of being alone. Neither felt obligated to make conversation so they sipped their wine and listened to the noise from the living room. They held hands and stared into each other's eyes for a long while until the simple connection wasn't enough.

"You look absolutely beautiful," Faye said, pushing Andi against the large mahogany table that filled much of the room. She buried her lips between Andi's breasts and fondled her.

"We really should get back," Andi said between kisses. "We've been gone awhile and I heard Mitch say Elise was going to open her presents soon. I know you want to see the look on her face when she opens that unicorn."

"We wouldn't want to miss that," Faye agreed. But instead of releasing her, she unbuttoned Andi's shirt and sucked on her nipples.

Andi moaned slightly and Faye quickly took advantage. She hooked her foot around the leg of a small step stool that Mitch used to reach the highest racks and brought it next to Andi.

"Step up," she said.

Andi obeyed and balanced on the tabletop. Faye hiked up her skirt and parted her legs. "You're mine." She kissed her deeply and massaged her thighs. "I want you."

Andi grabbed her wrists. "We shouldn't, baby. Not here."

Faye gave her a pathetic look. "C'mon, Texas. I've had a rotten week."

Andi sighed. "Oh, honey. I can't resist that," she said releasing Faye's wrists and laying on the tabletop.

Faye burrowed beneath her skirt, delighted by the purple thong Andi had chosen. Thank God she was a femme, she thought. She loved the rich creaminess of Andi's skin, courtesy of the expensive body lotions she religiously applied every day. And her legs were always waxed, another plus of dating a lipstick lesbian. She breathed deeply, savoring the incredible smell that was Andi. It was intoxicating.

With each touch they moved together. "I need you, honey. Please. I'm so wet," Andi cried.

She gasped at the first flick of Faye's tongue against her center. Faye knew she liked it slow and steady. She licked Andi as if she were a fine sorbet, savoring every juicy taste.

"A little faster, baby."

That meant she was close and Faye obliged. Andi's moans increased into a rhythmic cadence of pleasure until she hovered on the brink of climax, but an unusual sound joined in—the voices of a man and a woman.

"Faye, are you in here? I want to talk to you about this crazy gift."

And in the same second that Faye recognized the interruption, Andi sat up and both of them glanced toward the doorway, where Mitch and Elise stood, their mouths agape. In her hand Elise held the gold unicorn.

Chapter Twenty

"Good morning, Phoenix! Can you believe this is the last day of May? The summer weather is already here. We'll hit one hundred degrees by late afternoon, and for many Phoenix students, this is the last day of the school year. By tomorrow the kids will be flying off the high dives at our public pools—"

Constance silenced the squawking radio announcer with a quick swat of her hand against the clock's snooze button. She sat up and groaned. Her back was killing her, probably from the athletic sex she and Ira had enjoyed for the last five nights. She got out of bed and reached for her toes, visualizing each vertebrae and disc, knowing she should probably be practicing her Pilates daily. She rolled her eyes at the thought. How could she explain to her thirty-five-year-old lover that his old-lady girlfriend needed to stretch before they jumped in the sack?

The fact that he remained in her life was a mystery. She'd subjected him to all of her standard ploys for abandonment—long work hours, cancelled dates, her fiery temper, unreasonable demands and a haughty attitude. Yet nothing dissuaded him from continuing to see her. Only one other man had endured her horrible treatment for so long and he'd crumbled after meeting her secret weapon—A.J. After spending one afternoon with him at the zoo, the floral deliveries stopped and the phone calls dwindled to nothing.

She shook her head, unable to believe that *she* was calling and thinking of him by initials rather than his Christian name. Ira *liked* the nickname A.J. and had asked her to try it. So be it, she thought.

She breathed deeply and smelled bacon. She padded to the bedroom door and stuck her head out. Ira stood over the stove preparing breakfast, while A.J., who was already dressed, sat in front of the TV watching a *Mr. Zex* video.

"Come to the table, A.J.," Ira said.

She wasn't surprised when he didn't budge. He remained mesmerized by the cartoon character and ignored Ira's request. She wondered what Ira would do, which at first, was nothing. He calmly loaded the plates with food and she noticed that a tray sat on the counter with a rose in it. She smiled, realizing she would be served breakfast in bed.

Ira set two plates on the dining room table and went to the television. He turned off the set with the remote and stood in front of A.J.'s beloved fifty-five-inch plasma babysitter. A.J. whipped his head from side to side, unsure of what had happened.

"A.J., it's time to eat. Please come to the table."

He shook his head and pointed to the screen. "I'm watching *Mr. Zex.* I'll eat here." He patted the carpet next to him to indicate where Ira should set his plate.

She giggled quietly, already knowing how this little farce would end. Poor Ira. At this point she would have admitted defeat and allowed A.J. to gobble his breakfast on the floor while he remained glued to *Mr. Zex. Mr. Zex* always won.

"No, A.J. We eat at the table and it's time to eat. You need to wash your hands and come to the table."

She sighed. Ira had no idea what he was asking and how long it would take to coax him into performing both tasks— washing his hands *and* eating at the table. It would be lunchtime before the inevitable fight that was about to unfold was resolved. He had no concept of time and Ira already was glancing at his watch. She knew he had an eight o'clock meeting and it was seven fifteen.

A.J. pounded his fists on the floor and yelled. "You can't make me! You can't make me!"

Ira attempted to talk over his repeated chant, but realizing it was useless, he changed tack and went to the table. He sat in the guest's spot, for A.J. was adamant that people have assigned places, and began to eat his breakfast. She had indeed tried this ploy and it didn't surprise her when he stopped yelling and turned around to find his audience buttering some toast.

"This is really good," Ira said. "I heard scrambled eggs, bacon and toast was your favorite."

"White toast."

"Yup, it's white toast. And it's good. Why don't you come have some?"

"No!" he shouted and threw his whole body prostrate on the carpet.

She felt supremely satisfied. At least it wasn't her. Watching Ira employ the same strategies with little success reaffirmed her parenting efforts. She almost stepped out from her hiding spot to help him when he jumped out of the chair and stomped toward A.J. She opened her mouth to shout at him and defend her little boy, who she imagined was about to be physically assaulted by her short tempered lover. However when Ira reached for him, he gently wrapped his massive arms around his midsection and lifted him off the ground.

He was mesmerized and shocked. His jaw dropped and he extended his arms. She imagined that Ira would carry him to the table, so she was stunned when instead he twirled him in the air. After the third revolution he laughed heartily.

"Do you like flying like Mr. Zex?" Ira asked.

"Yes!"

He circled twice more and A.J. squealed in delight. He

stopped at A.J.'s place at the table. "Then you have to eat right now. Okay? And then we'll do it five more times."

"Yes!"

Ira twirled to the kitchen sink where A.J. scrubbed his hands, still dangling in the air. Then he twirled him back to his seat. He scrambled into his chair, grabbed his fork and began shoveling eggs into his mouth.

"Whoa," Ira said. "Slowly."

He obeyed. Constance turned away in search of a tissue. She didn't want Ira to see the tears streaming down her face. When he carried her tray into the bedroom, she had finished her makeup and was getting dressed.

"How can I serve you breakfast in bed if you're already up?"

"You didn't need to do this," she said weakly. "I don't have time." She went to her closet and chose her lucky blue suit.

"You need to eat."

"All I need is coffee and I imagine I'll need a lot of it today." She stripped off her negligee and reached for her bra, keenly aware that his eyes followed her every move.

He cleared his throat and sat on the edge of the bed. "What'll happen at the hearing?"

She joined him and rolled on her stockings. "The school will try to throw him out. They're already saying he's a danger and the little girl's parents are threatening to press charges if he stays."

"Can you blame them? He grabbed her breasts. That must have hurt."

She snorted. "Ira, she's twelve. She barely has anything to grab."

"That's not the point. How can you be so callous?"

"And how can you defend Faye Burton? He's mentally challenged. He doesn't mean to do these things."

"I'm not saying he does. There's no intent but that's not what this is about. It's about safety."

She froze and glared at him. "Maybe you should be the district's attorney."

He sighed and kissed her shoulder. "You know I want what's best for him."

She laughed. "You don't have any idea what's best for him. You've only met him a few times."

"And whose fault is that?"

She whipped her head around, confused. No man had ever *wanted* to spend time with A.J. She felt conflicted. The desire to throw her arms around him and sob was nearly overwhelming but she refused to release the anger and resentment that had built up during the course of his five-day suspension. She'd need it for the hearing.

Ira obviously saw the turmoil in her expression and took her hand. "Maybe he belongs at another school."

She jerked away. "You're either with me or against me, and right now you sure as hell aren't on my side. They may kick him out but I'll make sure they pay for it." She went to the bathroom and slammed the door behind her.

Faye Burton's curt secretary led Constance into the conference room and left without a word. She shook her head and sighed at the total lack of professionalism. She claimed an end of the conference table as a power move.

A sketchpad sat on the credenza next to her. A pencil drawing depicted a young girl next to an open grave, as if she was waiting for the casket to arrive. A pile of freshly dug dirt sat nearby, a shovel protruding at an angle. Wildflowers surrounded the graveyard, which bore a striking resemblance to the one where Cora rested next to their dead parents. Cora's funeral was the last time she'd gone home and the last memory she had of her sister.

After Constance moved to Phoenix, they had talked on the phone but she was too busy to go back and Cora obviously sensed her presence would be a burden. So while Constance climbed the corporate ladder, Cora waitressed at the same diner for twenty years. A.J. was the result of a short-lived affair with a married truck driver whose route conveniently changed after she told him about the pregnancy. Constance visited when A.J. was born. He'd seemed so perfect then and it took a few years before Cora and the doctors recognized that he wasn't developing at the right pace.

She picked up the sketchpad and stared at the young girl's face. She saw Cora. She blinked twice but she still saw her dead sister sitting at the grave.

"You need to take care of him, Connie," Cora said. "He's your flesh and blood."

"I will."

"Promise me you won't send him away. You won't put him in an institution. He'll die there."

"I know."

"Quid pro quo."

"Yes," Constance agreed.

The door opened and she quickly set the pad down and stepped away, expecting to see Faye Burton waltz into the room. Instead, a pretty dark-haired woman stuck her head inside.

"Excuse me but I left something in here." She pointed to the sketchpad and darted over to retrieve it before Constance could hand it to her. "I'm sorry to disturb you."

As she left, Andrea Loomis entered from the opposite door and nodded in Constance's direction. Right behind her was the regime of adults who intended to banish A.J. from Cedar Hills forever. Each person greeted her cordially but stiffly—the dreadful school psychologist, Mr. Nowicki, followed by Mrs. Strauss, Ms. Rasmussen and that other lesbian, Coach Fleming. Ms. Loomis directed each participant to a seat, carefully leaving the end chair—the other power seat—open. Loomis usually sat there and a red flag waved in her brain. Someone else would be attending.

Marjorie Machabell's overly exuberant and loud voice echoed through the neighboring corridor, announcing her approach. She entered, smiling and gesturing, with Faye Burton following. She immediately turned to Constance and extended her hand.

"How are you, Ms. Richardson. It's good to see you again, although I'm sorry that it had to be under these circumstances."

They greeted each other cordially with tight smiles. As she expected Dr. Marjorie took the other end chair across from

Constance, and Burton sat to her left, next to Loomis. They exchanged a whisper and she noticed the principal touched her colleague's arm as she made a point. Constance's lips curled into a slight smile at the familiarity. She had some surprises prepared for this meeting.

"We're all here," Dr. Marjorie said, usurping the control usually afforded to Loomis. "While it's certainly unusual for me to involve myself in hearings of this nature, I find this to be an unusual situation. So here I am," she said, almost cheerfully. "Ms. Burton, why don't you explain what has led to this hearing, which is also a Manifestation Determination meeting. For the record, a Manifestation Determination is held when a special education student commits a serious school infraction that could result in expulsion. This meeting must occur to see if A.J.'s actions derived from his disability. If we as a team believe they did, we must seek other ways to remedy the problem. Also, a natural discussion that will follow regards A.J.'s placement." She paused and looked at her. "Does this all make sense, Ms. Richardson?"

She offered a nod. "Yes, we've been through this process twice during A.J.'s educational career. The purpose is to determine whether his disability contributed to his actions and I'm certain we will find that they did."

She noticed everyone shifted in their seats at her editorial comments. She knew they wanted to use this opportunity to abandon her son—Cora's son—but she wouldn't let them do that to her family.

Burton looked at her notes and began reading. "On May twenty-fifth, A.J. was participating in his P.E. class. Coach Fleming was lining up the students and Jenny Kottmer passed by A.J., who stepped in front of her. He yelled fasty native and then reached up and grabbed both her breasts and twisted. She cried out and Coach Fleming ran over to assist Jenny."

"Was Jenny taken to the nurse?" Dr. Marjorie asked for the record.

"Of course. She was examined and her mother was called immediately. Physically she was fine but her parents have told me that she continues to talk about the incident and she's worried that A.J. will return to the class." Burton looked up from her notes. "Coach, do you want to add anything?"

She shrugged. "It was terribly disturbing to Jenny and the rest of the class. She started shrieking and A.J. was laughing. They didn't know what to think."

"I do have a question," Constance said. "Where were you? Were you monitoring the class?"

"Listen here, lady." The coach stood but Barbara Strauss motioned her back down. "I don't know whose idiotic idea it was to put that little boy in my class—"

"Actually it was the superintendent's," Constance said.

Fleming rolled her eyes. "Like I said, I don't know who the idiot was, but your son can't hack it in P.E. He's an okay kid but he doesn't belong there."

"Coach," Burton said, interrupting her while she took a breath.

The principal clearly didn't want her teacher to dig herself into a deep hole in front of the assistant superintendent but Coach Fleming didn't care.

"What? It's the truth, Faye. So try and fire me," she added, gazing at Dr. Marjorie. "I've got tenure."

Dr. Marjorie waved her arms, little conciliatory sounds floating off her lips. Constance recognized there were two hotheads in the room—Fleming and Burton. This could play to her advantage.

"And what about my son's injury?" she asked pointedly. "Clearly Mr. Salinas wasn't supervising him properly," she said, facing Faye Burton's deadly stare.

"The police officer who was called cleared Mr. Salinas of any and all wrong-doing. It wasn't his fault. Your son was naked and running through the office—"

"Let's try to keep this civil, Ms. Burton," Dr. Marjorie said with more force than Constance had ever heard. "Ms. Richardson is quite aware that Armour's behavior was unpredictable, and in fact, Mr. Salinas's actions most likely prevented Armour from further harm."

Before Constance could comment, Dr. Marjorie said, "Ms. Loomis, will you please lead us in the hearing?"

Loomis guided them through the routine questions about the incident, and then she paused, taking a deep breath. "The final question asks if this behavior was caused by A.J.'s disability and would a regular education student be inclined to do the same thing."

"No," Strauss answered emphatically. "It's unlikely that any other seventh grader would squeeze a girl's breasts in the middle of a class. And this action is definitely a part of A.J.'s impulsivity."

"I agree," Burton said. "We're back to the original question we posed at A.J.'s last meeting. Is this the appropriate setting for him? And I believe the answer is no."

"Actually, that's the next question, Faye," Loomis said, "but it does tie together."

Burton shrugged. "It's all semantics, Andi. The boy is a danger to himself and others if he remains at Cedar Hills."

Dr. Marjorie looked around the table. Constance noticed all heads were nodding and she imagined that Dr. Marjorie was the chosen messenger. "Well, it looks like most of the team is in agreement." She looked at Constance and folded her hands on the conference table. "Ms. Richardson, I know this must be a hard decision to accept but I must agree with these fine educators. We've given A.J. the best opportunities we could at Cedar Hills, but as is often the case with special education students, A.J.'s needs have shifted and this is no longer the appropriate setting."

"I disagree." She pulled out A.J.'s educational plan and dropped it on the table. "And according to this legal document, A.J. will continue at Cedar Hills for as long as I say."

Loomis cleared her throat. "Ms. Richardson, we understand your advocacy for A.J. but there's another matter to consider. Jenny Kottmer's parents have made it clear that if A.J. returns, they *will* press charges. You need to think about that."

Indeed she had but hearing Loomis say the words frightened her. From a legal perspective the facts were indisputable and A.J. was guilty of committing a crime. She'd already consulted with an attorney, and while she doubted the accusation would lead anywhere, she'd had a recurring dream where A.J. was standing in a prison cell. He was older, taller and much bigger, just like his father the truck driver who'd abandoned Cora. And now Constance was about to do the same—to save her reputation.

Tears pooled in her eyes, angering her immensely. This was not the time to show emotion. Her frustration crumbled into sadness and she reached deeper into her heart, to the anger she felt at Cora for dying and at Glen Oaks for refusing to help her any longer. Faye Burton would pay. She reached for the tissues that had strategically been placed near her at the beginning of the meeting.

"Where will he go?"

"I think it's time to move him to Arizona Behavioral Health," Loomis said gently. "They can address his academic and emotional needs."

She glanced down at the blank sheet of legal paper in front of her. She'd written down the date and time of the meeting but she hadn't made a single note. "How will this work?"

Loomis closed her notebook, signaling the end of the meeting. "I'll meet with the private placement specialist today and then my secretary will call you when we have an appointment made with the school, probably early next week. You and A.J. can come see the school and meet the director. Then he could start in the fall."

"Mr. Wilson, the director, is an amazing man," Dr. Marjorie added. "He's worked with challenged children for over three decades." Her eyes grew wide as she emphasized his credentials.

Constance remained still while everyone packed up around her. Rasmussen, Strauss, Fleming and Nowicki quickly left. For them this meeting was a slight interruption, a note in their PDA. She doubted they truly recognized the impact of their decision. Now she would endure the fallout, arguing with A.J. each morning as she tried to prepare him for school and spending hours at night answering the same mundane questions about why he'd left Cedar Hills. It would be exhausting and it would devour huge amounts of her precious time that could be used as billable hours.

Loomis finished her conversation with Dr. Marjorie and glanced at Constance. "Ms. Richardson, before we break do you have any other questions for us?"

She had many but none they could answer. She had decided, though, that if her life would be uprooted, she'd enjoy some company. Quid pro quo.

"I do have one question. How can this decision be legally binding when there is so clearly a conflict of interest?"

Suddenly the levity in the room disappeared

"Pardon me?" Loomis asked.

She leaned forward and locked eyes with Loomis. "I'm suggesting that your judgment is clouded because you're sleeping with Ms. Burton. I imagine that A.J. is a constant topic between the two of you, given that I am a huge pain in Ms. Burton's proverbial ass." She chuckled slightly and folded her arms. "I'm very concerned that this decision is based on your personal feelings rather than your professional judgment. Dr. Marjorie, would you care to comment? I imagine Dr. Gleeson would find this information quite interesting."

She let her words sink in before she savored their reactions. Dr. Marjorie's mouth moved slightly but couldn't form words. She glanced at Loomis, who looked as though her dog had just been shot, and then at Burton. Her face was beet red and Constance imagined she was angry to the point of violence.

"How dare you inject such innuendo," Burton said. "You have no right to bring up anyone's personal life in a meeting such as this."

Constance raised her index finger, prepared to give a legal lesson. "Ah, but I do. There is much case law that discusses conflict of interest and in many Supreme Court cases the court has found that defendants have grounds for legal redress if their case was handled unfairly. I believe this to be the case with my son. You want him gone and Ms. Loomis has agreed to do your dirty work, regardless of his needs."

Burton shook her head. "You are truly the most despicable woman I have ever met." She rose and went to the door. "I can't believe you. I don't understand how you can have so little regard for A.J. or other children. Your selfishness is unmatched. Maybe it's because he's not really yours," she added, as she flung open the door and exited.

She nearly flew out of her seat at Burton's parting shot but she caught herself and gripped the arms of the chair. Her eyes dropped to the conference table, rage surging through her. At least she didn't feel sad anymore.

She turned to Dr. Marjorie. "I'd like an answer to my question. Are you concerned about conflict of interest?"

"I am not." Her eyes never wavered but her hands were shaking slightly. She recognized the seriousness of the accusation for the school district.

Savoring the moment, Constance pushed the manila envelope into the center of the table. "You're not concerned or you don't think I have any proof of a lesbian relationship between two of your administrators?"

Dr. Marjorie's expensive foundation couldn't hide the frown lines that crept on her face. She remained stoic as she examined the pictures but her eyes gave everything away. When she looked up, she sighed.

"Ms. Richardson, I don't understand what you hope to gain by throwing this red herring into the discussion. A.J. needs a more restrictive environment. Can't you see where this is headed? If he continues to act out sexually, he'll be arrested and you could face charges as well."

She swallowed hard, the prison dream filling her head.

"I know it will be difficult for him to adjust to a new school but better a new academic environment than the penal system." She set her hands on the table and smiled sympathetically. "You gain nothing from this sensational announcement. Let's stick to the issue for his sake."

She'd infiltrated her paranoia and tickled it. Underneath her suit jacket she knew her Dior blouse was plastered to her back, beads of sweat telegraphing her panic. Her mind shifted to Burton and Loomis. How many nights had they lain together in bed, complaining about their workday and Constance Richardson? Wouldn't their jobs be so much easier if she and her autistic son were someplace else?

She gathered the pictures and set them neatly in a pile in front of her before she said, "If you insist on continuing with this placement, I will be forced to expose this conflict of interest to the governing board and the media."

From across the table Dr. Marjorie's expression turned stony. "It would not be wise of you to make threats or give ultimatums to me." She spoke softly but with great strength. There was no tremor in her voice now and her hands had stopped shaking. "I spend more time working for the Glen Oaks School District than I do with my family. This district *is* my family and I will protect it. If you push *my family* into a corner, we will have no choice but to defend ourselves, and as a *family* law attorney, I don't believe you would relish publicity that would cast doubt on your abilities as a mother."

A slight smile crept over Constance's face. She couldn't help it. She enjoyed battling a worthy opponent and Dr. Marjorie had surprised her.

"I certainly appreciate your concern for my professional livelihood but I believe we are at a stalemate. How would you suggest we resolve it?"

Dr. Marjorie's warm smile returned. The laugh lines settled in place and Constance imagined that she much preferred the role of pleasant diplomat—unlike herself—who lived for the kill.

"Maybe we can find some middle ground."

Chapter Twenty-One

Pandy wandered down the hallway to Ms. Clark's office. She glanced through the conference room window and saw Ms. Richardson surrounded by a ton of people. She guessed they were talking about what A.J. did to Jenny. Sonia had told her about it and she thought she could have prevented it. But she'd been out of school for over a week, ever since the day of the yearbook party. She hoped A.J. would get the help he needed or he'd turn into a guy like Travis—or worse.

She knocked softly on Ms. Clark's door and peered inside. Ms. Clark was on the phone, but when she saw her she smiled broadly and motioned for her to come inside. Pandy sat on the big couch and noticed her sketchbook on the chair nearby. She wrung her hands and bobbed her legs up and down nervously. What would Ms. Clark think of her drawings? She'd never shared them with anyone but she thought she might be going crazy.

She only remembered pieces of the afternoon in the ceramics court. She'd gone into shock, at least that's what the doctors had called it. They'd given her pills and let her grandfather take her home but she'd just lain in her bed for two days. Ms Clark was there sometimes talking to her. Eventually she got up. It was like walking out of a fog.

She'd reached under her bed for her special box, the place where she kept her razor blades, but it wasn't there. She looked throughout her room and noticed many things were missing—her scissors, the sewing kit her grandmother had given her, even her pencils were gone. Every sharp object had been removed and she felt an overwhelming sense of relief that she couldn't explain. She was *glad* they didn't trust her and she knew she didn't trust herself. It was nice to be taken care of for a change.

She'd leaned against the sink in her bathroom and her grandfather appeared in the doorway, his hands in his pockets. His hair was snow white and every wrinkle on his face cut deeply through the skin. Pandy imagined she'd aged him plenty since she'd arrived.

"You're not gonna do anything stupid, are you?" he asked.

She shook her head. What could she do? "No, Gramps."

He nodded slowly and stared at his shoes. He turned to leave and stopped. "You know, Pandora, I've never given you any advice, never thought I had a right, given how your mother turned out. It's not like we did so great with her. Hell, I'm awful with words anyway." He sighed and looked at her thoughtfully. "I just know that we don't get to pick. We get stuck with the life we get and we choose what we do with it. I know you'd rather be with your mom but you don't get to pick." He shrugged. "You're stuck with this old man."

He ambled away, favoring his left leg. Pandy could tell his arthritis was bothering him. She knew he worked too hard as a mason, and if it wasn't for her living there, he could probably retire. She followed him out of her room and watched him trudge down the hallway. It was a sight she would carry with her for a long time, a symbol of his sacrifice. She smiled and felt wiser. And loved.

"Hey, that's a nice smile," Ms. Clark said.

Pandy blushed. "I had a really good conversation with my grandpa the other day."

"That's great." Ms. Clark joined her on the couch and gave her a hug. "I was so worried about you."

"Thanks for everything you did."

Ms. Clark waved off the compliment but Pandy knew that when they took her to the hospital, Ms. Clark had stayed there to make sure that her grandfather wasn't overwhelmed. Then she'd helped take her home and Pandy imagined it was Ms. Clark who'd cleaned out the house of all the dangerous objects.

"Is it true you got married?"

Ms. Clark grinned. "Yes, but you'll still call me Ms. Clark, okay?" She gave her a friendly pat on the knee. "How are you doing? Are you ready for promotion tomorrow?"

"Yeah," she said, although she couldn't have cared less. She was only participating in the ceremony for her grandfather and Sonia.

Sonia had visited every day and she found herself longing for the afternoons when Sonia raced over after school. They talked about all of the gossip surrounding Pandy's attack. Apparently people believed Brian shot Travis, stabbed Dylan and put Sean in the kiln.

Pandy wasn't surprised. They had to make up something when the gay girl and the A-list boys didn't show up for school the next day. Of course the truth was much simpler. After hearing her story, which Sean supported, Principal Burton suspended Travis and Sean for the rest of the year and wouldn't allow them to participate in promotion. Dylan was still in the hospital with a fractured skull but was expected to recover. Brian had been taken to a special hospital and Pandy wondered if she would ever see him again. He was in big trouble with the police.

She glanced at her sketchbook and flipped through it until she found the page she was looking for—the single drawing where she mentioned Athena. It was the only one in all of her sketchbooks where she wrote Athena's name. She hadn't expected Ms. Clark to peer over her shoulder that Saturday when they worked on the mural. How odd was it that Ms. Clark had seen this drawing? A shrink would tell her that she wanted someone to see it. She wanted to tell someone what happened.

"Pandy, who's Athena?"

Pandy gazed into her eyes and saw honesty and warmth. The corners of her mouth tugged into a sad smile. She looked down when she said, "My baby sister."

Ms. Clark squeezed her hand. "I didn't know you had a sister."

She nodded. "She was eight years younger than me."

"Did you guys have the same father?"

She shook her head. She had no idea who Athena's father had been. Her mother told her stories about Athena's father, a dashing mechanic who'd worked at the garage in town until he found out his girlfriend was pregnant. Then he'd suddenly disappeared.

"You've never mentioned her."

No, she thought. How could she explain this? It was hard enough to say her name. She already felt as though she'd breached a sacred trust. Her mother would never want her back now.

"Pandy, did something bad happen to Athena? Is that why you never talk about her?"

An enormous lump formed in her throat and she wished it would suffocate her. It would serve her right. It would be payback.

"She died."

She looked down and stared at the swirls in the blue carpet. She couldn't see the beginning, only the ending and Athena's still little face and body.

"It happened because of the wildflowers," she blurted, realizing that wasn't right. It sounded stupid. Athena didn't die because of flowers. "Well, no, I guess there was important stuff before that. Stuff about Mama."

"What kind of stuff."

"I always felt sorry for her. She worked all week and had to pay for Athena to go to daycare. Sometimes she had to work double shifts for that. On weekends she just wanted to have fun."

"What did she do?"

She shrugged. "You know. She partied with guys like Uncle Harry."

"Where did they go?"

"To the Bum Steer."

"Is that a bar?"

"Uh-huh."

"Where were you?"

"I was babysitting Athena."

"How old were you when you started babysitting Athena at night?"

She searched her memory. "I think I was nine and Athena was about one. Before then Mama said I was too young. I wouldn't know what to do with a brand-new baby."

"I see," Ms. Clark said quietly. "How long were your mother and Uncle Harry gone?"

She had no idea but she knew it was the middle of the night when they came home after she'd fallen asleep on the couch and long after she'd put Athena to bed.

"Late," she said.

She and Athena had a routine every Saturday night. After her mother and Uncle Harry left around six she'd make some macaroni. They ate a lot of macaroni. Then she'd clean up the kitchen, give Athena a bath, watch a kids' video and get her ready for bed. She'd sit in the old rocking chair and read her a story before she put her in her crib. After Athena went to bed she would lie on the couch and watch TV. Her mother and Harry usually woke her up when they came home. They were always giggling and groping at each other. She'd pretend to be asleep and Mama would put a blanket over her while Harry grabbed another bottle of bourbon and headed for Mama's bedroom. Eventually Pandy would hear the squeaks from the bed frame and Mama's low moans. She knew what was happening. She'd throw a pillow over her head until morning, drowning out their sex sounds.

"What was it like being an older sister?"

Pandy smiled. "It was great."

"Did Athena ever wake up while you were babysitting? You know, because she was sick or upset?"

"Only once. Mama always gave her some medicine to help her sleep when I babysat."

When Ms. Clark raised an eyebrow, she wished she hadn't mentioned it. She could tell Mama wasn't sounding so great in this story.

"So what happened the one time she woke up?"

"She had this terrible cough. She sounded like a seal."

Ms. Clark nodded. "She had croup, right?"

"Yeah. I didn't know what that was then. I tried rocking her, feeding her, giving her the pacifier, a whole bunch of stuff. I even gave her another dose of the medicine but nothing worked. It was so hot that night. I walked around the trailer, bouncing her in my arms. That usually helped her go to sleep. I just remember it was so hot and my arms got tired. I finally had to call Mama. I was really worried."

"And what happened?"

"She came home. She was mad."

"Was she drunk?"

She nodded slowly. "She grabbed Athena and took her in the bathroom while she kept yelling at me. I went into my room so I didn't have to hear it."

"Was Athena okay?"

"Yeah, after she went to the doctor."

Ms. Clark patted her knee. "It sounds like you had a lot of responsibility for your sister, especially considering that you were pretty young yourself."

"I was old enough," she said quickly. "At least I thought I was."

"How did she die?"

She closed her eyes. An enormous gust of wind seemed to sweep across her face as she thought of that afternoon. It was breezy and the wildflowers swayed from side to side like they were dancing.

"It started with the wildflowers. They grew all around the trailer and they were taller than Athena. She could barely walk and she'd grab onto them to keep her balance when she was outside. That day Mama and Uncle Harry left early. They went to the bar to watch the NBA playoffs around three. Athena and I were still outside when they left. We played and hung out. I thought I saw a raccoon and I chased him away. When I turned toward the trailer, I saw that Athena was toddling around the back. She fell into a huge puddle and covered herself in mud.

"I scooped her up and took her inside. I knew she was dripping mud on the carpet and Mama would scream if she saw it. I got her into the bathroom and out of her clothes. She still didn't talk much but I could tell she was happy. She kept smearing the mud all over herself and laughing."

Pandy started to cry and Ms. Clark handed her Rocco, the funny looking giraffe that she kept in the office. Pandy squeezed him tight and sobbed into his plush fur. She couldn't stop herself. She heard Athena's laughter as if she were in the room.

"Did you give her a bath?" Ms. Clark asked.

"I filled the tub and set her in it. I handed her the yellow ducky and she made him squeak. She seemed fine and I couldn't stop thinking about the mud. I had to get it up. Mama would flip when she saw it. So I got Athena situated and left her there squeaking her ducky while I ran to the laundry room and got a few cleaning supplies—"

"You left her alone in the tub?"

"I checked on her every few minutes and she was still sitting up. I kept hearing the squeaking, over and over. I'd get some of the mud up and then I'd run into the bathroom. She was laughing and squeaking her duck. I checked on her again before I ran the vacuum. I definitely wanted to vacuum up the rug shampoo before I got her out of the tub. Athena always cried when she saw the vacuum."

"So what happened next?"

"I ran the vacuum and then the phone rang. It was Mama, asking how everything was going. Ever since the night Athena caught croup, Mama made a point of calling and checking in. I told her everything was fine and she asked me some more questions, but it was hard to hear because everyone in the bar was yelling and cheering, and Mama was slurring her words pretty bad. We hung up and I started to put the vacuum away and then I realized it was too quiet. Athena wasn't squeaking her duck. I ran into the bathroom but I couldn't see her from the doorway. I went to the tub and she was under the water. The duck was over in the corner as far away from her as it could be. I pulled her out, hoping she'd take a breath, but she was like a doll. I kept saying her name and talking to her. I put her on the rug and tried to do CPR but I really didn't know what I was doing. I couldn't get her to wake up so I called nine-one-one. The lady tried to help me over the phone but it wasn't working. It seemed to take forever for the paramedics to get there."

"Did you call your mother?"

She shook her head. "I just kept trying to do the CPR. Then I hear feet tramping up the steps and voices calling to me. This huge fireman is in the doorway and grabs Athena off the floor and takes her into my bedroom. I watch all these other men and women rush past the bathroom. Then this female firefighter comes in and sits down next to me. She asks me what happened and where my mother is..."

"And what else?"

She thought of the pretty firefighter with beautiful blue eyes. But when they'd looked into hers they'd been filled with tears. "I started to cry. I knew." Then the firefighter held her close and she felt safe. It was the best hug she'd ever gotten.

"I hear this awful scream and I run to Mama. The firefighters are trying to calm her down. She calls for me and I run to her but when I hold out my arms she smacks me across the face."

"What?"

"She was drunk. I've always thought about that. I guess she blamed me. I know I did."

Ms. Clark paused and took a deep breath. "So what happened after your mother hit you?"

"A fireman grabs Mama by the arms and she starts flailing around, crying and screaming. She calls out for Athena and she calls me the b-word. When she spits on me, the fireman pulls her away. The police come and they put her in handcuffs. The female firefighter holds me again. I'm shaking. I'm not crying. I was just shaking."

"Where did you go?"

"Social services let me stay with a friend and they called my grandfather. He came and got me a few days later."

"What happened to your mother?"

"The court said it was an accident. She had to go to counseling and AA and the judge decided I should stay with my grandparents."

"Did you go to Athena's funeral?"

She shook her head. "No, I was gone by then and Mama was still angry with me. I've never even seen Athena's grave."

"Would you like to?"

"Uh-huh." She buried her face in Rocco's long neck. "I miss her so much," she cried.

Ms. Clark held her tightly. It felt as good as the firefighter's hug that day long ago. When she stopped crying, Ms. Clark gently pulled Rocco away from her and put her hands on Pandy's shoulders.

"I want you to listen very carefully to me. What happened to Athena was an accident. You were put into a terrible situation by an alcoholic who didn't use very good judgment. It was a tragedy but you've never forgiven yourself, sweetie. That's why you cut yourself and that's why your sketchbook is filled with those drawings. You're such an awesome girl and you have so many gifts. We're going to work on letting this go and I'm going to recommend that you see this friend of mine who's trained to help kids who've been through this kind of stuff. Okay?"

She smiled weakly and wrapped her arms around Ms. Clark. She listened to her heartbeat, steady and even. Whenever Mama had hugged her, it'd always seemed to be for Mama, not her. And Mama's heartbeat sounded like pounding drums. Pandy closed her eyes and sighed. Maybe it would be okay.

Chapter Twenty-Two

Faye shot past Pete's office and tore into her own, slamming the door. She had to get out of there. She knew if she returned to the meeting she'd say something entirely unprofessional. She couldn't imagine how Andi was feeling and she dreaded to think of the ramifications to their relationship. A picture of Thelma and Louise going over the cliff flashed in her mind.

Pete came in while she was shutting down her computer. "I won't ask if you're okay. That would be dumb. What can I do to help?"

She grabbed her briefcase. "I need to go."

Pete nodded. "Fine. Go buy a six-pack and get shitfaced."

He left and she headed to the back exit and her car. The conference room doors were shut, which meant Marjorie was still sorting through the fallout. She passed the empty office at the end of the hall and found A.J. glued to the TV watching *Mr. Zex*. They'd obviously stuck him in there as a way of keeping him close for the meeting, one that he technically was required to attend by law but couldn't because of his current disruptive nature.

He sat in an office chair, his hands folded behind his head. She almost laughed at his pose, which reminded her of a powerful executive. All he needed to do was put his feet up on the desk and he'd be ready for Wall Street—except for the spaghetti sauce covering the front of his shirt and the snot running out of his nose.

She leaned against the doorway and glanced at the screen. She'd never seen the show and she couldn't understand the appeal. Mr. Zex was a blue zombie who seemed to be accompanied by a sidekick named Morty. A.J.'s mouth hung open in full concentration while Mr. Zex and Morty braved the grocery store. Suddenly Morty jumped into the cart and Mr. Zex wheeled him madly through the aisles, eliciting screams from Morty and hysterical laughter from A.J. After turning into the produce section, Mr. Zex lost control and the cart careened into a display of bananas. Morty crawled out of the rubble and spun around.

"Fascinating!" he cried.

On cue, A.J. crawled on the desk, twirled exactly like Morty and screamed, "Fasty native!"

Fascinating. Fasty native. She laughed and A.J. glanced in her direction, his eyes growing wide. He quickly climbed down and returned to the office chair.

"Sorry, Ms. Burton. Please don't turn off *Mr. Zex*."

"Don't worry, A.J. I'm not going to turn it off. Just stay in the chair, okay?"

He smiled broadly and nodded furiously. Mr. Zex barked at Morty and A.J.'s head snapped back to the screen. Faye trudged through the back door and saw Constance Richardson sail out the front entry, power walking toward her car. The few minutes with A.J. had cost her a quiet exodus. Constance had her Bluetooth attached to her ear and she was chatting away. She saw Faye and stopped immediately.

The sidewalks converged and a confrontation was inevitable unless they childishly ignored each other. Faye approached her and she finished her conversation, disengaging the phone apparatus.

"Ms. Burton, it's unfortunate you left the meeting. I'm sure Dr. Marjorie will be speaking to you soon."

"I imagine so."

"You got what you wanted even though it will come at a high price to you personally. A.J. will be transferred from Cedar Hills."

She was grateful that A.J. would finally get the help he needed but she couldn't hide her irritation at the outcome. She imagined she and Andi would be reprimanded for conflict of interest and it floored her that a parent had leveraged her professional future, using homophobia as a crowbar.

"Ms. Richardson, I do have a question for you."

"What is it?" she asked impatiently.

"You know that phrase A.J. says all the time, fasty native?"

She sighed audibly. "Yes, I do. It drives me crazy."

"How often does he say it?"

She snorted. "At least twenty times a day. If he becomes extremely agitated, he'll repeat it. Once he said it for an hour."

"Wow. That sounds really annoying."

"You have no idea. The doctors say it could be some sort of code. If they could unlock its meaning, they might understand him more."

"So you don't know why he says it? After all these years of living with him, acting as his advocate, sharing all that precious quality time, you're still in the dark about your son's secret?" Constance's expression withered and Faye thought her lips trembled. "After claiming to know what is best for him, even against the advice of educational experts, you still don't know why he constantly uses that phrase or what it means."

Her cheeks reddened and her eyes narrowed. "No, I don't."

She grinned. "Well, I do."

She heeded Pete's advice and picked up a six-pack at the Circle-K nearest her house. She wasted no time stripping off her clothes and turning on the hot tub. She opened the first beer and put on her iPod to block out the world. The jets spun over her tight muscles and Lucinda Williams' melody asked, "Are You All Right?" The answer was clearly no but she cracked open her second beer and allowed a midafternoon buzz to overtake her. It wasn't even three o'clock.

Her brain flooded with concerns about her job. Constance had implied she would face some sort of disciplinary action and she cringed when she thought of her career resting on the shoulders of a twelve-year-old.

"And I thought Bill Gleeson would be my undoing," she mumbled.

Ironically this issue wasn't about A.J. at all and Faye knew it. Constance had pandered to every school district's greatest fear—poor PR. Homosexuality remained the greatest taboo and parents secretly worried that gay educators would brainwash the youngsters, transforming them into muff-diving, fudge-packing homos who couldn't read or write but yearned for sex.

Her logic seemed flawless after three beers. She heard the back door close and Andi crossed the lawn, still dressed in her power suit. She fell into the lounge chair next to her and sighed.

"Wanna beer?"

"Absolutely," she said, popping the cap. She downed half of it in three swallows and leaned back, kicking off her dress shoes. She tilted her head to the sky, letting the sun warm her face. Faye gazed at her perfectly delicious neck and had an urge to jump out of the tub and shower her with kisses.

"Honey, we need to talk," Andi said.

Her amorous mood immediately evaporated. "About what? The meeting? Us? The district? There are so many topics from which to choose."

"Don't be sarcastic, okay? There's too much shit here."

"Pick your shit, Andi. What do you want to talk about?"

"Well, let's start with the meeting. After you ran out and left me to deal with Marjorie and Constance, the two of them really got into it."

"Catfight?"

Andi slapped her thigh. "Damn it, Faye. This is serious."

She sighed. "Go ahead. I won't interrupt. I know you're pissed because I left you there with them. I—"

"You're damn right I'm pissed. You get to make some huge exit and take a parting shot at the parent while our personal lives are thrown onto the conference table and Constance attempts to blackmail the district—"

"What?"

Andi nodded. "Constance said that if we didn't keep A.J. at Cedar Hills, she'd go to the media and expose our affair—"

"How in the hell would she do that?"

"She had pictures."

Faye was stunned. Never before had anyone executed a vendetta against her. She didn't believe the pictures were incredibly damaging since Andi insisted they always maintain a platonic distance in public.

"So what did Marjorie say when she saw them?"

"To her credit Marjorie didn't back down. She actually pushed back a little. She insinuated that if all of this came out in the media, Constance's career would be affected too. She was adamant that A.J. needed a different placement and eventually Constance agreed."

She shook her head. "Okay, but what's the price? This is Constance Richardson, the pit bull attorney. She didn't give in for free."

"No," Andi said softly. "She kept saying quid pro quo. Marjorie's a politician if she's anything. She knew that some sort of remuneration was the only guarantee she had to silence Constance about us."

She stared at Andi. "What kind of remuneration? Letters in our files?" Andi couldn't meet her gaze. It was worse. "So are we fired?"

Her eyes dropped to the ground. "Not me. Just you. Well, you're not fired, of course," she quickly added. "The district's not going to renew your contract. They'll exercise the at-will clause and they'll find someone else for Cedar Hills."

Faye shook her head, the fury inside her growing. "Why do

I get to resign? Why not you?"

Andi didn't answer right away but instead drained her beer and reached for another. "Truthfully, I think they like me more. I'm the team player. I'm the one—"

"Who looks straight."

"That's not the reason, Faye."

"The hell it isn't!" She pulled herself out of the hot tub and threw on her robe. "Andi, you're the perfect little worker and if it weren't for me, no one, and I mean *no one*, would ever suspect you're gay. And that's exactly what the Glen Oaks School District wants. If it's a competition between the two of us—the frumpy dyke principal in her sensible shoes or the stylish and coiffed director in her power suits and designer pumps—I will always lose. And the worst part is that there's nothing I can do. I can't fight this. I can't scream to the Office of Civil Rights or to the government. I'm not a protected class. I'm being discriminated against and it's *legal*."

Andi stood and faced her. "I know, baby. I know it sucks." She reached for her but Faye stepped away. "C'mon, babe. This isn't my fault. This isn't about us."

"That's easy for you to say," she snapped. "You're still employed."

Andi crossed her arms and glared at her. "I'm not the enemy, Faye. Don't do this."

"Do what? There's nothing for me to do except maybe go out and buy some heels," she added.

Andi wagged a finger at her. "Listen, missy, you know damn well I don't dress this way to hide. I actually *like* wearing makeup and shoe shopping. And I thought *you* liked the way I look."

She threw up her hands. "I do like the way you look but it's incredibly convenient for you too." She sighed heavily, feeling the effects of three beers. "So when am I supposed to learn my fate? If I go read my e-mail now, will there be a summons from Marjorie?"

Andi took a deep breath and said, "She's not going to tell you."

"You're kidding me. *This* is my notification? You're the hatchet man? I can't believe this. I thought you were here as my caring lover, not to do the assistant superintendent's dirty work."

Andi wiped a tear from her cheek. "She thought you'd rather hear it from me given the sensitive nature of the conversation."

"What? Dyke to dyke? And you believe that? She can't even give me the courtesy of a meeting?"

"I'm sorry, Faye. I really am."

Faye's eyes traveled down her perfect body, adorned with beautiful makeup, an Anne Klein suit and expensive pumps— and she knew.

"Shit. She made you a deal, didn't she? She promised not to tell Gleeson about you if you agreed to can me." Andi said nothing and couldn't meet her gaze. "I'm right, aren't I? He's so superficial that he'd never suspect you were a lesbian. Someone would have to tell him outright. Great way to protect your own hide, Texas," Faye drawled sarcastically.

"Damn it, Faye! That's totally unfair. I thought I was doing you a favor. Okay, it helps me too. I'll concede that. But why in the hell would you ever want to sit in another meeting with Marjorie or that idiot Gleeson? He's so stupid he doesn't know whether to scratch his watch or wind his ass."

Andi was right. Gleeson had been gunning for her since they met and this situation was convenient ammunition. The thought of him taking secret pleasure in dismissing her made her sick. Yet Andi never should have agreed to be the messenger. That was self-preservation. She'd put her career ahead of their relationship.

Faye grabbed the last beer and huffed into the house, slamming the back door a little harder than she meant. The house shook and a ceramic pot, one Andi had bought for her while they were on the cruise, fell off the window ledge and crashed onto the tile. She exhaled, thinking that by nightfall, ever-organized Andi would have sent her an e-mail detailing a plan to exchange their stuff.

She fell onto the couch and began to process her feelings but she quickly decided it didn't matter. Relationships were so rarely worth the trouble. At least she'd figured it out before they'd done anything as foolish as live together. She took a long pull from the beer and made a mental list of all the careers for which she was qualified.

Chapter Twenty-Three

Constance debated between the cabernet and the merlot and decided on the bolder, firmer 1986 Pahlmeyer cabernet in honor of the day's accomplishments. She poured a glass and settled onto the sofa, folding the silk robe around her. She wore a lavender baby doll nightgown beneath it—Ira's favorite. She'd slipped some CDs into the player, including a collection of Brahms' piano sonatas, and the living room suddenly transformed into an adult playground. All she needed now was her playmate, and he would be arriving soon after a late evening appointment with a new client—a woman he assured her was no competition.

When A.J. had learned that Ira was staying over and in the morning there would be white toast and helicopter rides, he readily picked up all of his toys and took them to his room before climbing into bed.

She savored the wine and contemplated the bond that had quickly developed between them. Perhaps it was because they were both little boys in different ways. She chuckled and leaned back into the plush sofa, confident that Ira wouldn't appear until she'd consumed most of the cabernet, enough for a pleasant buzz to suffocate the fear of inadequacy that seemed to manifest itself whenever they made love. He said he liked her in sexy lingerie but whenever she stood in front of the mirror, she saw the wrinkles, the cellulite and the sags that telegraphed her age. Was he blind?

Relationships were her Achilles' heel. She knew that. Her career was her salvation and today she'd gained the upper hand against the Glen Oaks School District, thanks to that unbelievable narcissist Marjorie Machabell. She should have stopped the meeting and called the district's attorney but the woman was too proud and now they'd pay.

Faye Burton was history and Constance imagined Burton's resignation could shatter her relationship with Andrea Loomis, a fact that made victory that much richer. The only moment that tainted the day was learning that Burton had cracked A.J.'s secret world. Perhaps she was bluffing but Constance didn't think so. For the right price maybe she would reveal the meaning of fasty native.

There was also the issue of A.J. changing schools. Constance dreaded telling him. Perhaps Ira could do it. A.J. seemed to like him almost as much as that ridiculous Mr. Zex. She pushed aside the annoying particulars that she knew would work out.

She never bothered much with details because that really was where the devil lay. Her mother had always told her to watch the big picture and forget the rest. As an attorney she'd hired the best paralegals and secretaries who soldiered over the minutiae and ensured that every pleading was top-drawer. She needed that help. She didn't have the patience to read every word of a deposition or listen to the simple-minded testimony of witnesses who were the linchpins to a case.

Sometimes, though, it was important to notice the little things and she'd learned that from her sister. Cora was the one who paid attention to details. She always ironed the tablecloth or stacked the canned goods by height, and while Constance couldn't see the point of such drudgery, Cora's compunction for exactness kept the family from falling apart.

After their mother died it was Cora who saw the gradual changes in their father, not her. She recognized his visits to the pub occurred more frequently and he stayed longer. He would come home drunk and over time he developed a violent streak, one Constance didn't understand until the night he hurled a book at Cora's head and smashed her mother's mirror instead. When he saw the shattered pieces of glass glistening against the hardwood, he fell to his knees and sobbed. Constance stood there while Cora silently retrieved the dustpan and broom. At that moment it was finally clear to Constance. Their father had died with their mother and the family was destroyed.

The night he broke the mirror was a turning point. She and Cora veered down a dangerous road with their father, who grew more brutal as the months passed. At sixteen Cora insulated her from the arguments and the beatings. It was Cora who met him at the door most evenings after he staggered home and wanted to fight. Constance would lie in bed, the covers over her head, ignoring the shouts and Cora's pleas that penetrated the bedroom door. Inevitably there was a slap and she would retreat to their room and lock the door behind her. She'd crawl into bed with Constance, who would hold her hand until she fell asleep.

One night Cora didn't meet their father, and instead she hid in the bedroom too, attempting to escape another bruise on her cheek. The girls realized their mistake after he came home and found himself alone in the living room. He broke their door down and yelled at the top of his lungs. Terrified, they rolled out of bed and against the wall. He paced the room, screaming and sobbing, calling their mother's name.

"June!" he wailed incessantly until Constance's head pounded from the noise.

She thought when the effects of the liquor diminished his tirade would cease, but the yelling and the pacing went on for over an hour, and she stayed huddled on the floor, pretending to be somewhere else. At one point he grabbed a knife from the kitchen and waved it in the air, fighting an invisible enemy. She feared for her life and wondered if they would live to see morning.

"I'm going to try something," Cora whispered. She went out to the living room and Constance crept to the door and peered out.

Her sister advanced toward their father, slowly and timidly. She stepped in his path and his mouth closed in mid-scream.

"Buck," she said calmly. He stared at her with crazy eyes until she touched his cheek. "It's all right, honey. I'm here."

His expression melted and tears streamed down his face. "June," he said, "I thought I'd lost you." He pulled Cora into a fierce embrace, his hands squeezing her buttocks and his mouth covering hers.

Constance was sick at the sight. She watched her father, certain that some sliver of recognition would cross his face and then disgust would follow. Instead he smiled broadly.

"I'm so glad you're here. C'mon, baby."

He took Cora's hand and led her into his room. Cora glanced over her shoulder, fear in her eyes. Constance heard the lock click. She strained to hear what was happening on the other side of the wall but there was nothing except an eerie peace. She didn't return to the bed, unwilling to bundle underneath the covers without Cora, thinking it was unfair for her to lie in comfort while her sister endured—it. Her eyelids grew heavy and she fought to stay alert but sleep overtook her, and when she awoke it was daylight and Cora lay in the bed. Constance climbed in and wrapped her in an embrace. She heard Buck moving in the kitchen, filling the coffeepot with water, pouring cereal in a bowl and closing his lunchbox.

There was a sudden knock on the door and he stuck his head into their room. "You two sleepyheads better get up. You'll be late for school."

Gone were the wild eyes of the night before. He smiled slightly before shutting the door again. Cora blinked awake and gazed at Constance.

"Oh, Connie," she sighed, her voice cracking. "I'm sorry."

She shook her head. "What have you got to be sorry about? It's his fault."

"He can't help it. He misses Ma."

She was dumbfounded. How could Cora defend him? "The fact that he misses Ma is no excuse. It's wrong. It's *sinful*."

Cora sat up and held her by the shoulders. "Listen to me. You may be right but if you tell anyone, they'll take us away and we won't be together. That's what'll happen if they find out."

"Really? We'll leave?"

Cora nodded. "Yes. I'm making my own decisions and I'm going to protect you. I know what I'm doing. I just pretend I'm with Arnie." Arnie was Cora's current boyfriend and the first boy she'd taken to bed. She kissed her on the cheek. "He'll never touch you—ever. I promise."

And he hadn't. Cora had continued to sacrifice herself whenever their father's delusions sent him into a rage, which seemed to be about once a week. Afterward Cora would return to their room and Buck never remembered anything the next morning.

The ritual continued for three long years until fate mercifully closed the tavern—the only one within walking distance to their house. Buck's father had been killed by a drunk driver and he was too petrified to drink and drive. Once Dunphy's closed he stayed home and drank alone, unaware that Cora was doctoring his whiskey with a sedative that her friend, a pharmacist's assistant, was providing. Instead of flying into a rage he fell asleep every night in his chair and didn't awaken until morning. Finally their nightmare was over but Cora's dreams of Hollywood had died as well.

She had stayed in Atwood to protect Constance from their father until they could both leave, but by the time Constance graduated from high school, she'd convinced herself she would never be famous. Their father had stolen her dream and robbed her of her dignity. Instead it was Constance who left and pursued her own dream and it was all because of Cora's willingness to place herself between Constance and their father. When cancer claimed Cora, Constance assumed responsibility for A.J., just as Cora had assumed responsibility for her.

"Quid pro quo," she said out loud.

The click of the CD player signaled the end of Brahms

and the system whirred until it changed to a Wynton Marsalis collection. She refilled her glass and staggered to the bookshelf, the expensive wine compromising her sobriety. She found the small picture of Cora next to the thick volume of Shakespeare's complete works. It was a professional black-and-white head shot, taken by a photographer who readily slashed his fee in half for a chance to sleep with a beautiful budding starlet. She stared at the picture. Cora looked amazing. Her smoky eyes and seductive smile would have equated to success in Hollywood. Constance was sure of it.

The door opened and Ira appeared, his hair disheveled and his tie askew. For a split second she almost yelled at him for intruding and then she remembered she'd given him a key. That was a first. She smiled slightly at the man who was her polar opposite. She said nothing as he stripped off his jacket and tossed it and his briefcase into a chair. She would never do that and until he'd entered her life she would never have permitted a man to be so slovenly in her presence. For some reason he was different and easily forgiven.

His eyes roamed her body and the open robe. "Very nice," he said on his way to the kitchen for another wineglass.

When he returned to the living room, she'd replaced Cora's picture on the shelf but she couldn't take her eyes from her sister's glamorous face. He pressed against her back and kissed her neck.

"How'd it go today?"

"Fine," she said. "He has to change schools."

He turned her around. "And you're okay with that? I thought the point was to keep him at Cedar Hills."

A smile crossed her face. He still had so much to learn. "No," she said. "The point was to win and I did. There was a change of strategy. I think the new school probably will be better for him."

He shrugged. "I don't get it."

"It's quid pro quo, darling. You never get anything for free. They wanted him to leave so I agreed but not without a price."

He raised an eyebrow and poured some wine. "Do I even want to know?"

She drifted into his arms and kissed him. "No. Now do you want to make love to your cougar?"

He laughed. "You are *not* a cougar. That would imply that you preyed on me and caught me like a defenseless animal."

"I did."

"You only think you did. I *let* you catch me. I let you think you're in control. I let you treat me like shit."

The truth of his words took her aback. She was drunk and not a single witty retort escaped her lips. All she could say was, "Why?"

He held her face between his strong hands. "Because I see what you're feeling. I see the way you look at A.J. I watch your eyes mist over every time you talk about your sister. I don't listen to the bullshit words you say and I don't believe your steamroller PR. You let me in, darling, and I know that probably scares the hell out of you but it's too late. I'm already here."

Shaken, she stepped away and reached for her wineglass. Once she'd drained the expensive cabernet, she said, "So does this mean you expect some happily ever after crap?"

He laughed again and dropped onto the sofa, his loafers carelessly landing on the expensive cushions. She was repulsed and started to say something until she saw his grin.

"It's killing you, isn't it?"

He flipped off the shoes and extended his long frame to its full length. If he grabbed the remote, she was certain he'd turn on a football game and demand a beer.

"What the hell do you think you're doing?"

He made a show of gazing around the condominium before settling on her. "Getting comfortable."

He motioned for her to join him but she stood her ground, glaring at him. Their eyes locked and she felt his goodness wash over her. It was redemptive. Her arms fell to her sides and she went to him, a tentative smile on her face.

Chapter Twenty-Four

The sun crept overhead and Pandy felt the summer heat scorch her bare shoulders. She rapidly moved her paintbrush over the wall, determined to complete the black outline before the paint congealed and forced her to quit. Sonia followed behind, filling in the arcs of the rainbow with the bright colors that would re-create the mural. Once in a while they would look up at the same time and smile or giggle. This was Pandy's idea of heaven, combining the two things she loved the most—art and being with Sonia.

The school year was over and Pandy wasn't even a student at Cedar Hills anymore but Ms. Burton had asked her and Sonia to repaint the mural after everyone was gone.

"I thought we couldn't redo it," she'd said to Ms. Burton.

Pandy knew Ms. Burton was leaving too and she couldn't

understand why it was so important. Neither of them would be there to enjoy it.

"I know that's what we said, Pandy, but I think it needs to be done."

Ms. Burton had smiled mysteriously and she felt like she was getting away with something, something forbidden. When Ms. Burton told her to invite Sonia to help, she'd instantly accepted the challenge of re-creating the same design that had been defaced by those idiots Poncho and Turtle.

"It feels weird to be here without anyone else," Sonia said, picking up the can of yellow.

Pandy glanced around the empty courtyard. "I kinda like it. I mean we're not totally alone. Ms. Burton's in her office finishing stuff and some janitors are here."

"Yeah, but we're the only kids. You know?"

"Yeah."

She stole a look at Sonia who stretched to reach the top of the rainbow with her paintbrush. Her pink tank top pulled away from her denim shorts exposing most of her midriff. Pandy stared at the copper skin. She loved touching Sonia's body although their make-out sessions were still pretty innocent. She hadn't shared the secrets of her past with Sonia but she wanted to, and she made a mental note to phone Ms. Clark and ask her opinion.

Ms. Clark had insisted she call once a week during the summer to check in. They'd spent hours on the phone and Pandy told her all about her sessions with Naomi, her new therapist. Ms. Clark sounded so happy and she'd also promised they'd go shopping. This is what it must feel like to have an older sister, Pandy thought.

And she was going to Utah with her grandpa to see Athena's grave and visit with her mother and Joe—but it was only a visit. She'd accepted that her life was here with her grandfather. He was even going to therapy with her sometimes. They were a team and things seemed better now that she knew she could count on him. Of course he'd always been there for her but she hadn't been paying attention. That's what Naomi had taught her.

"We're probably gonna have to stop," Sonia said. She showed Pandy the thickening green paint. "This stuff's just coming out in globs."

"Okay. I'll just finish outlining this last part. Then we can quit."

Sonia smiled. "What do you want to do for the rest of the day?"

She shrugged. "We could go swimming at your house."

"Yeah, let's do that but at two I have to go to Xavier to meet my new coach. She's having a summer volleyball clinic next week and the doctor says my arm's well enough to play."

During the attack Sonia had sustained a hairline fracture to her wrist but she was healing quickly. Since promotion they'd spent every day together, watching DVDs, hanging at the mall, swimming in Sonia's pool and best of all making out in Pandy's room. They avoided talking about the fall because they wouldn't be attending the same school. Sonia had received a scholarship to Xavier College Preparatory, a school with a strong volleyball and swimming team. Pandy would have to suffer at Central, the neighborhood high school. She wasn't excited about it until Ms. Clark learned there was a gay teen group on campus. Then Pandy thought it might be bearable. She'd miss Sonia and she imagined that once the school year started they would go their separate ways and that was okay.

She stepped back to look at the mural and Sonia's arms circled her middle. "It's really coming along," she said. "You are so unbelievably talented. You should be a professional artist."

She eyed the work critically. "I think it looked better the first time. It's like there's something missing. I just can't figure it out."

Sonia disagreed. "It looks the same to me."

She scanned the mural and settled on the lower right corner. "No, it's missing the peace sign over there."

"Oh, yeah. I forgot about that."

She squatted and pulled the paint cart close to the wall. "That's because it wasn't memorable. It was cliché. Even Ms. Taylor said so."

She stared at the blank space of wall. Something needed

to be added or once again the entire mural would be out of balance. An idea came to her—something better than a peace sign.

Without bothering to create an outline she painted two girls on the wall, one with beautiful blond hair and the other with short, spiky brown hair. The blonde sported a cute blue skirt and pink tank top while the brunette wore a black T-shirt and black pants. They were smiling and holding hands.

Sonia started to laugh. "Oh, my God! Are you really going to leave us on the mural?"

Pandy stood and stepped away to see her work. It was obvious they were girls, and although the drawing was located in a lower corner, it was highly visible.

"Yeah. Let everyone know we were here. It's better than a signature."

Sonia laughed and took her hand. "When Ms. Burton sees that she'll probably order the custodians to paint over it."

Pandy remembered Ms. Burton's smug smile when she'd asked her to repaint the mural. "No," she said, "I don't think she'll mind. I think she's gonna love it."

Chapter Twenty-Five

"If you insist on selling furniture it would be much more sensible to have a stall on the first floor," Rob said with a grunt as he maneuvered his end of the stuffed divan into the elevator.

Faye ignored the comment and joined him inside for the ride up. She knew it was a pain to cart furniture upstairs but she liked her location—a corner stall that had an additional five feet of space because of a niche that the builders had added.

They rearranged some of the other large pieces to make room for the divan and once she was satisfied with its placement, they plopped down on the cushions to rest.

"Thanks, bro," she said. "I couldn't have done it without you."

"You wouldn't need me if you'd call Andi."

She scowled. He'd once again thought of a way to inject her into the conversation. It was true that she was amazingly strong and she'd often joked about her country roots, but they were done as far as Faye was concerned. She just needed to convince Andi, who for the past three weeks had left voice mail messages and sent flowers. Faye secretly harbored some regret, wondering if she was making a mistake, but it was easier not to look back. She was keeping herself busy with job applications and planning a rafting trip down the Colorado River with friends.

"When do you and Jonnie leave for Alaska?" she asked, changing the topic to his honeymoon.

"On Saturday. So I hope this is my last job as moving boy."

"It is. It'll be slow for the next six weeks or so." She looked around at the stall. It was as full as it could get and sales fell off during the summer. Her eyes settled on a small, framed picture on top of a credenza. "God, will she ever give up?"

She showed him the picture of a little cowgirl on a wooden pony.

He studied the photo. "Where'd you get that?"

"I didn't. Andi left it here for me to find. It's the third time she's planted a photo. The first one was of the two of us on the cruise and the second was her high school graduation picture."

He laughed. "Well, that's creative. She's absolutely adorable in this picture. You're lucky nobody tried to buy it." He nudged her and she cracked a grin. "How cute was she at eighteen?"

"Okay, I'll admit she was gorgeous but she's got to let this go. We broke up. She needs to come and get her things out of my house and stop leaving stuff in the stall."

"I'm supposed to tell you that Jonnie and I think you're making the biggest mistake of your adult life by dumping the most intellectually challenging, beautiful and funny woman you've ever dated."

She nodded. "So noted. Now, can we stop talking about her?"

"Fine. How about lunch?"

She sighed. "I can't. Believe it or not Elise has invited me to lunch at the country club."

His eyes widened. "I take it you're speaking again?"

"Sort of. We haven't really talked to each other since the party. She just left a message on my phone and asked me to meet her for lunch."

"That party was unbelievable," he laughed.

Rob had reported that after Faye and Andi dashed out of the house, Elise had found the rarest bottle of French wine Mitch owned and drank it in ten minutes. She then rejoined her guests and insisted that Lindsay's old karaoke machine be brought in from the game room storage closet.

"Her rendition of "Heard it through the Grapevine" was really quite good," Rob said, remembering that night.

Faye was sorry she'd missed it but Alec had caught much of it with his video camera and promised to make her a DVD.

When Rob stopped laughing he said, "Lunch, huh?"

"Yup. Now that I'm a lady of leisure I can enjoy such frivolity."

He glanced at her cargo shorts and Indigo Girls T-shirt. "Just be sure you change into an appropriate frock," he advised, pointing his nose in the air. "If you're rubbing elbows with the elite you can't be wearing deadly dyke attire."

The dining room of the Scottsdale Country Club was packed with members enjoying their Tuesday lunches. She was stunned by the number of people casually dressed in the middle of a work week. They'd obviously figured out a way to avoid traditional labor and she wished she knew their secret. Once she secured a teaching position she'd be lucky to get lunch except in summer.

Many of the guests sported tennis whites, having just come from the courts, and she chastised herself for having rushed home to change into Dockers and a button-down shirt. If they could wear their sweaty tennis clothes, she could don her concert T-shirt.

She found Elise sitting at a table in the middle of the room, chatting with the waiter who'd just brought her a martini. Faye felt better about her wardrobe choice when she noticed Elise dressed in a peasant blouse and skirt. She studied her sister until Elise looked up and waved her over.

"What do you want to drink?"

"I'll have a Heineken."

He disappeared and she settled in the seat across from her sister. As usual Elise looked perfect. Her hair was clipped by a black barrette and she wore a hint of makeup. Even though she was nearly ten years older she'd always looked younger than Faye.

"Well, how are you? How's the job hunt?"

"I'm fine. I think I might go back into the classroom. I'm not sure I want to be a principal anymore."

"Wouldn't it be a terrible cut in pay?"

She smiled at how quickly her sister honed in on the financial implications. "It's not always about money, Elise."

Elise's cheeks reddened and she started to respond and then shook her head. "We need to talk. Since my birthday I've really worked hard to understand everything. I met with Jonnie and Rob—"

"You guys had a meeting about *me*?"

Elise threw up her hands. "Faye, I don't know you. I'll admit that. You were always so close to Rob and I was always left out. I'll admit I was a little jealous."

"You were jealous? We were jealous of you. At least I was."

Elise looked stunned. "Why?"

"You were...well, perfect."

Elise rolled her eyes and sipped her martini. "Please." She set down her drink and stared at Faye. "Why didn't you tell me you were gay?"

"I've thought about that a lot. I guess I didn't want to be disappointed in you and I was sure I would be. It's like putting a book down because you think you know the ending and you won't like it. So you just avoid it."

"I've never done that," Elise said. "I give the author the benefit of the doubt."

She shrugged. "Touché."

"Am I really that bad? Do you hate me?"

She was taken aback and momentarily speechless. How many times had she made jokes at Elise's expense and she could never explain her "Ding, Dong the Witch is Dead" ring tone if Elise ever heard it. Did she hate her sister? She automatically shook her head.

Elise stared at the tablecloth. "Are you sure? I mean it's okay if you don't like me. We don't get to choose our families."

"I guess I don't really know you."

When Elise looked up there were tears in her eyes. "Thank you for saying that. You *don't* know me but I'd like us to change that."

"I guess I've avoided you because we're so different. I can't imagine what we have in common other than the same parents."

Elise paused, clearly thinking this over. "Let's see. I like fine wine, old movies and rainstorms. Any of those?" she asked hopefully.

Faye had to smile. At least she was trying. "I can't tell the difference between good and bad wine, I'd rather see an action movie and rainstorms depress me."

Elise nodded and raised her glass. "So I guess we'll just have to keep thinking."

"Why did you move back to Phoenix?" Faye asked suddenly. She had no idea why the question popped out. "Was it for your job?"

Elise was disarmed momentarily. She only shook her head.

More curious than ever, Faye pressed. "Then why?"

The waiter dropped off Faye's beer and Elise waved him away when he asked if they were ready to order.

"Mom was sick, remember?"

Faye nodded. Their mother had been diagnosed with ovarian cancer when Faye was twenty. Amid her pain and grief that lasted three years as they watched her die, she'd never connected her mother's terminal illness with Elise's homecoming.

"I didn't realize—"

"You never thought I cared about Mom. You always thought I was Daddy's girl."

"No, of course not," she replied.

Faye sipped her beer, surprised at the direction of the

conversation. She wasn't sure what else to say and she wasn't sure she wanted to know the truth. She'd written her own version years ago.

Elise gazed out the window toward the golf course, her mind lost in the past. "Mom was frantic after the diagnosis. Dad didn't leave her much in the divorce and her insurance was a joke. We thought Mitch could help her navigate the system if we were closer. And the bills..." Her voice trailed off and Faye knew what was coming.

"The short version of the story is that Mitch took a job at Mayo and I went to work as the vice president in the new Phoenix office of the company."

Faye remembered her mother's weekly visits to the Mayo Clinic. She'd asked her how she could afford it but her mother had provided vague answers. Now she knew—Mitch's connections and Elise's money.

"So Elise saves the day," she said out loud.

"And that's exactly why I never told you," Elise said sharply.

I am a rotten sister, she thought. She stared at Elise with complete sincerity. "I'm sorry and thank you for helping Mom. Does Rob know?"

She shook her head. "We've never spoken of it."

Faye couldn't process everything at once. She knew she'd spend the next several days thinking of the past, realizing her entire perception of Elise was flawed.

"Here's to Mom," she said, raising her beer bottle.

They toasted and Faye noticed Elise's attention drift behind her. She wondered which of Elise's tennis cronies would be joining them.

"So have you spoken with Andi?"

She stared at the expensive china plate before her. "No."

"So are you avoiding her just like you've avoided me?"

Faye shook her head, willing away the tears that surfaced every time she thought of Andi.

"No? Well, let's find out."

Faye turned and saw Andi coming toward them. She wore a hesitant smile and a floral sundress that revealed a decent amount of her cleavage. When she arrived at the table she didn't immediately sit down, although Faye realized there were three place settings.

"Hey," she said, a trace of her Texas drawl creeping out.

Faye took a deep breath. Andi looked fabulous and she felt herself being pulled into those gorgeous eyes. "Hi. What are you doing here?"

"I invited her, Faye," Elise quickly said. "It wasn't her idea. She came to me and explained everything. She's brokenhearted."

She shot her sister a wary glance, well aware that meddling was one of Elise's strongest traits. If Elise believed something was good for you, it was.

"And who the hell are you? You've only known I was gay for about ten minutes. Now you're an expert on my love life?"

"No, but I do know something about relationships. Don't forget I've been with the same man for over twenty-three years. You and Andi—"

"There's no Andi and me," Faye said abruptly.

"Please don't say that, baby," Andi pleaded. She pulled the third chair close to Faye and sat down next to her, taking her hand. "I'm so sorry about what happened. I got scared and I should've stood up for us. I see that now. If you want me to quit, I will. We can drive right over to Gleeson's office and I'll plant a wet one on you right in front of him." Faye chuckled slightly and Andi stroked her cheek. "There's the smile I love. Don't say we're through, baby, please. I don't accept that."

It was so easy to get lost in her eyes but Faye shook her head. "I can't, Andi. We're too different. I don't care what people think and you spend your life looking over your shoulder."

Andi reached into her purse and withdrew several pieces of stationery. "I'd say my life is about to change. This is a letter to my folks. I'm going to tell them who I am and I want to tell them about us. I want there to be an *us*."

She stared at the paragraphs of Andi's flowing handwriting, reading snippets of sentences that revealed Andi's true self and her undying love for her parents.

"Are you sure you want to do this? Your dad's sick. Is this wise?"

Andi shrugged. "I don't know. I just need to do it."

She heard Andi's words but they wavered on the fence of sincerity. Faye wondered if she'd really mail the letter or get cold feet. It was hard to come out to anyone but she couldn't imagine telling a sick parent, especially one who'd spent his whole life living in a right-wing small town.

"It'll never work out," she heard herself say. She rose and grabbed her bag.

Andi's face tensed and she slammed her hand on the table, rattling the crystal goblets. The sound quieted much of the restaurant and several patrons turned to gawk. "Damn it, Faye. I love you, even if you are a stubborn jackass. I'm sorry I let Marjorie manipulate me. I shouldn't have been the one to tell you about your job." She turned Faye around so they faced the other patrons in the restaurant. "So you think I can never be as out as you are, huh?"

A gasp tore through the restaurant when she pulled Faye into a deep kiss. When they broke apart, Andi whispered, "I love you, honey. This is real. Do you feel it?"

Faye was speechless. It *was* real and she couldn't picture another day in her life without Andi. "Yes," Faye said, kissing her softly. "I do feel it."

Andi grinned. "Good. Now, let's have some vittles with your kinfolk."

They sat down and when Faye looked at Elise, she expected her sister to be mortified. She was certain Elise would immediately abandon her budding friendship with Andi and she wouldn't speak to Faye until Rob played peacemaker, if then. She remembered the great blowup of two thousand when Bush was handed the election. After a vicious argument where Elise said the Supreme Court was right, they hadn't spoken to her for six months.

She expected to see the same expression now, but when their eyes met, Elise smiled. She didn't gaze about the dining room, assessing the judgmental stares of her friends and charity colleagues—for many of them were whispering and pointing—but instead she turned to Andi.

"Andi, what would you like to drink?"

"Elise, I believe I'll have a seven and seven."

Elise motioned to the waiter and placed the order before returning her gaze to Faye. "What's the matter?" she asked, clearly amused.

"Don't I look shocked?"

"Yes. And your mouth is hanging open as well. You may want to do something about that."

"What's happened to you? Where's my uptight Republican sister?"

"I'm not sure." She took a sip of her martini and glanced at Andi before returning her stare to Faye. "I probably should be in heart failure since your lesbian girlfriend has just declared her love for you and kissed you in the middle of my country club. Despite this fact I am calm. I have not passed out, my Republican sensibilities are not offended and I am not prepared to spout off some homophobic comment. Mitch doesn't need to sedate me and neither my voice, nor my blood pressure, is raised." She picked up her menu and put on her reading glasses. "Now, I strongly recommend the salmon."

Within minutes Andi was asking Elise about her handbag and the two of them were planning a trip to Nordstrom's. Faye sat back and watched the exchange as an outsider, as she would if Elise was a parent at her school. She hung no frame around her sister's picture but judged her for her own merits. And she liked what she saw.

When the check was paid, or rather when the check was put on Mitch's tab, they walked to Elise's SUV, gossiping about Jonnie and Rob.

"They seem really happy together," Andi said.

"Yeah," Faye agreed. "They're perfect for each other. I should've seen it."

"Still," Elise said, "Vegas? Couldn't they have waited?"

Andi put an arm around Elise and gave her shoulder a squeeze. "That's the point. They didn't want to wait. They wanted their happiness right away."

Elise nodded, obviously accepting the logic. "Well, I should be going."

Faye turned to her sister and gave her a hug. "Thanks for lunch."

Elise pulled her closer. "I love you, sis."

"Me too, you."

She stepped away and opened the SUV's hatch. "There is one thing. I do have my limits. I can accept Jonnie and Rob's shotgun wedding, and I'm thrilled that my lesbian sister has chosen such a wonderful girlfriend, but..." Her voice trailed off as she withdrew a fancy paper bag. She pulled out the tacky unicorn and held it up. "I really want us to be closer but not like this." She shook her head. "You have to take this back."

Faye laughed and took the unicorn. Elise got into the SUV and started to back out. Suddenly, she stopped and rolled down the window as if an idea had just come to her.

"Maybe after you move in together you could put it on a special shelf."

Faye almost dropped the statue but Andi caught it before it slipped through her fingers. "Move in together?"

Elise looked perplexed. "Isn't there some joke about lesbians and U-Hauls?" She shrugged, waved and drove away.

Andi wrapped her arms around Faye's waist. "Your sister has a point. We're way past the third date mark." When Faye looked panicked, Andi chuckled. "You're so funny, baby. You look as scared as a cat at the dog pound." She hugged her tightly and kissed her. "We'll take it slow. I think we need a vacation. What about Cancun?"

They held hands and walked across the lot toward Faye's truck. "You've forgotten that I'm unemployed with no prospects in sight yet. And if I go back to teaching, we'll be vacationing in my backyard."

Andi squeezed her hand. "You'll find something. I hear there's lots of math openings. Maybe we could rent a cabin up north for a long weekend?" Andi suggested.

Faye's cell phone rang and she didn't recognize the number on the display. "Hello?"

"Ms. Burton, this is Constance Richardson."

She almost hung up but curiosity overrode contempt. "How did you get this number?"

Andi's eyes widened in surprise at her tone.

"That's not important and I assure you that I have no intention of hounding you in the future. I am calling because I have an important business proposition for you."

"Really? What business could we possibly have to negotiate?"

"You piqued my interest the last time we spoke. You claim to know what A.J. means when he blurts out that ridiculous phrase."

Fasty native. Of course. That was her angle. "Yes, I'm quite sure I know why he says it."

"And would you care to share that with me?"

"Not particularly."

There was a long pause and Faye imagined that most people when faced with a long pause from Constance Richardson caved to her demands. She remained silent. She was no longer the principal whose duty was to serve parents.

"I see," she replied. "I respect your position, Ms. Burton. Quid pro quo. Absolutely. I'll offer you five thousand dollars to explain the meaning of this phrase so long as I believe it is the *true* meaning."

Faye bit her lip. The idea of spending another moment in her presence almost wasn't worth the money—*almost*. "I'll come to your office in the morning, Ms. Richardson. We can make our exchange then. Please have the money in cash. I'm absolutely positive I know."

"Fine," she said primly. "I'll see you at nine."

Faye closed her phone and stared at Andi, who was shaking her head. "What could that woman want with you now? Hasn't she done enough?"

The midafternoon light glistened against Andi's hair and Faye's eyes traveled down her perfect body. She knew she was staring at the woman she loved and would never let go. A seductive smile crossed her face.

"What?" Andi asked, her eyes dancing.

"What are you doing for the rest of the afternoon?"

She stepped closer to Faye until their lips were almost touching. "I don't know. What am I doing?"

"I think we should go shopping. How do you feel about wearing a bikini?"

"Why would I need a bikini to go to the mountains?"

"Change of plans, baby. We're going to Cancun."